TO
CARRY
A
BODY
TO ITS
RESTING
PLACE

AMID THE VASTNESS
OF ALL ELSE SAGA
BOOK FOUR

TO CARRY A BODY TO ITS RESTING PLACE

C.S. HUMBLE

SHORTWAVE PUBLISHING

Cover and interior design by Alan Lastufka.

First Shortwave Edition published July 2025.

10 9 8 7 6 5 4 3 2 1

ISBN 978-1-959565-68-0 (Paperback)
ISBN 978-1-959565-69-7 (eBook)

Amid the Vastness of All Else Saga

That Light Sublime Trilogy

Book 1 – The Massacre at Yellow Hill

Book 2 – A Red Winter in the West

Book 3 – The Light of a Black Star

The Peregrine Estate Trilogy

Book 4 – To Carry a Body to Its Resting Place

Book 5 – San Antonio Mission

Book 6 – The Baroness of the Eastern Seaboard

Josh Rountree

Welcome to the Peregrine Estate.

Some of you are new around here, soon to discover what the Peregrine Estate is, and to bond with the selfless and capable people who comprise its ranks. Others of you are old hands. You've read the *That Light Sublime* trilogy and taken it into your hearts.

Now if you're new to all this, don't fear. These novellas stand tall, and they stand alone. These are epics in miniature, each one a beautiful and violent glimpse into the wider world that C.S. Humble has created.

And for those of you, like me, who closed the last page on the *That Light Sublime* trilogy, desperate for more? This is exactly what you were hoping for. These books take us to so many places we longed to visit. Are you interested in those rumors of werewolves, or eager to shoot your way up the ranks of The Gunfighters Guild? Have you wondered how Judge Ellison enlisted so many fierce and interesting folks into his ranks?

Were you wishing for a just a little more time with some of your favorite characters?

Well, here they are.

You'll soon recall what a fierce friend Sarah Lockhart is, and you'll come to understand the family dynamic that informs the seemingly misguided actions of the broken, but determined, Ashley Sutliff. Within these pages you'll witness the kindness and love that lies at the heart of otherwise violent men like Sven Erickson and Larry Cornish. And you'll ride alongside Gilbert Ptolemy on a mission of righteous vengeance.

Might be, you've met these people before. But you're about to understand exactly who they are.

Don't ask me for details. I'm certainly not here to spoil any surprises.

But know this: the *Peregrine Estate* trilogy exudes the same strengths as every other C.S. Humble book. His wonderful gift of *emotion*, and his almost supernatural ability to create characters we bond with in an instant.

You won't just read these books, you'll *feel* them.

There's a reason Humble's *That Light Sublime*

trilogy developed such a devoted following that goes far beyond his talents for immersive world-building and breathless plots. We truly bond with his characters. They form a community in our mind that's inclusive in a fashion we don't often attribute to the "Old West." Humble strives for diversity in a way that is evident in every scene, and brought to life in vivid detail.

He allows his characters to breathe. Shows us the quiet, human moments that remind us of ourselves and our own private battles. We are all imperfect souls striving for our own brand of personal transcendence, and Humble under-stands this. He invests his characters with these same sorts of struggles. He grounds them in their strengths and their weaknesses, and asks that we bear witness to their fraught relationships, long ago forged from love, and hate, and lesser calamities of the heart.

We see the true faces of the world in Humble's fiction, and are better for it.

And when these friends we've come to care for make terrible decisions, we understand exactly why they're doing it. We figure, under those same circumstances, we might make the same poor choices.

That's where the stakes come in. In Humble's fiction, there are few second chances. Bad decisions lead to consequences. When the violence comes, and it *always* comes, nobody is escaping without a few scars. Life is precious, and one bad move can strip away everything we love.

That is not to say these books are grim in any way. There is an enduring earnestness to Humble's stories that always leaves space for hope and joy, and I think that's another element of his secret sauce. In a world that increasingly shows how little humans care for one another, C.S. Humble shows us just how much he *does* care.

There's a kind of magic in that. And it's written into every page of this remarkable trilogy.

Welcome to the Peregrine Estate.

—Josh Rountree
November 15, 2024
Georgetown, TX

For George R.R. Martin

A hell of a writer. Hell of an inspiration. A fevered dreamer if ever there was one.

PART ONE

ONLY FOR A PIECE,
ONLY FOR A TIME

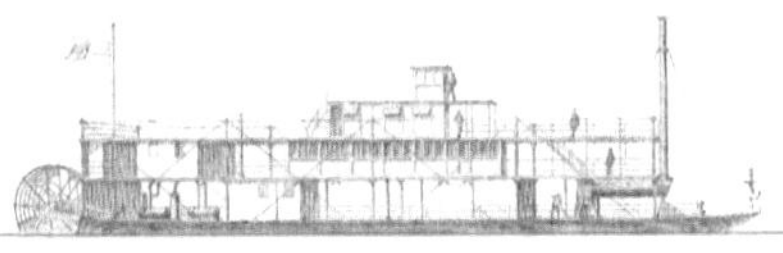

CHAPTER ONE

THE BLIND CROW SALOON
ST. LOUIS, MISSOURI
JANUARY 8, 1845

I t was in the winter of Ashley's Sutliff's nineteenth year when his brother, Willow, walked through a set of snow-powdered St. Louis saloon doors and, without offering salutation amid the low, smoky lamplight slanting across saloon girls and card-holding gamblers and cowhands alike, said simply, "Daddy's asking you to come home."

Ashley Sutliff, in mid-hand and absent of all desire to travel back to the hog farm, much less speak to his father, drew out his rejoinder, long and dramatic. "Well, hello, dear brother. As you can see, I am currently preoccupied with success." He looked up from his cards, the rest of him unmoving, giving his brother a hot-eyed stare. "Winning at the life Daddy said would only lead to ruin. So, you will understand me when I say: Fuck off. Go home. Let me gamble."

Will, half-a-head taller than any other man in the room, reached up and removed his ridge-top hat. Like the man, it was powdered with snow, rumpled, marked by more than the weathering of its years. And Ashley saw what the shadow of the mud-speckled brim had been hiding. What he had not heard in his brother's voice. There were tears in Will's brown eyes. Tears and the silent resignation only seen in the absolute surety of an oncoming tragedy.

Ninety-nine times out of a hundred, Ashley would have japed his brother and cussed him in front of this gambling cohort. He was that kind of man, priding himself on his meanness and brusque manner. But, made a witness to the pain in his little brother's face, Ashley was compelled toward that one in one hundred moment. An unwritten compact, composed by the blood in their hearts, bridged the silence between them, altering their lives forever.

Ashley rose and said to the gamblers surrounding him, "Gentlemen, I have urgent business at home. But I assure you, I will be back, expecting my due from this full house you all thought I was bluffing."

He splayed his cards among the mess of chips: two kings and three nines, set before four groaning men and a dealer grinning like a Jack.

"Put it on my credit, Charlie," said Ashley to the dealer, a smooth-shaven man wearing a French silk shirt and red vest, fancy as you please. "I'll spend it all on whiskey and gals soon enough."

"Ain't no way," said a beady-eyed elephant of a man seated to Ashley's right, gripping his cards so tight they seemed to wither like flowers in a drought. "There ain't no goddamn, mother-fucking way you slow-played a full house. Not the way you've been throwing your chips in with deuces and fives and stole a pot on a goddamn pair of threes."

"And yet. . ." said Ashley, smirking, palms up. He realized he'd forgotten the man's name. Was it Wilbur? Willard? No, it was Walter. He was sure of it. There was no need for things to get crazy, no reason for tempers to flare. And so, Ashley put a hand on the big man's shoulder and squeezed. "No hard feelings there, Walter, I—"

The corners of the man's mouth lifted, exhuming an expression set between a snarl and the nose catching the aroma of horseshit. "Who the fuck is Walter?"

"Ashley," said Will, still standing in the cut of the saloon door. "I will not suffer to wait."

"You'll fuckin' wait until I get what's owed me," said the big man. "This little shit is a cheat if I've ever seen—"

"A what?" Ashley snapped.

"Ash—" Will started.

"A fuckin' cheat, I said."

"Aw, shit," said Will, resigned.

"A cheat," said Ashley, nodding. Eyes widening as he accepted the inescapable detour set before him and his journey home. And thus, Ashley sprang from his seat while cocking the right hand that had broken noses and shattered the eye socket of a Louisiana mule-skinner not six months back, and let it fly with all the destructive power living within him.

The blow struck the big man in the face. The other two gamblers at the table scrambled, the dealer, too. Ashley threw himself as a pile of fury atop the man, smothering him with blows—overhands and hooks, slaps and eyerakes. Ashley might have given up a full grain-sack worth of weight to the gambler, but when it came to the melee distance between them he refused to give an inch.

When Ashley was a boy, his father had educated him on the tempo and insistence of violence. "Once you get on top, you waylay until they lay still. Don't quit if they beg. Don't stop if they're hurt. Unless someone pulls you off, you hit a man enough times so he can't remember the fight but will never forget what you did to him."

The big man had wagered to call Ashley a cheat, and that gamble would prove—

"Ashley," Will's voice called from a far-off place, calm and cold, cutting with command.

"Christ," cried the big man, toppling out his chair, his face slapping hard against the grimy floorboards. He lifted massive balled fists around his head, wailing for the help of a god that would not answer. Would not intercede.

Every eye watched. None of the witnesses moved.

Ashley kicked one of the man's hands away and, knee first, dropped his full weight on the man's wrist. There was something like the sound of an old tree limb giving way. The big gambler howled.

Satisfied with the sound, Ashley howled right back, eyes and mouth stretching wide, a jester made a lunatic by a joke that has driven him mad.

"Ashley," Will said again.

Undeterred and wild with rage, Ashley set one thumb over the other and wrapped his fingers around the big man's throat. Though he had been away from the hog farm for two years —away from the setting of fence posts and the tossing of hay bales and the hammering of ten-thousand nails that sunk head-deep on a second strike—the holding of cards had taken none of the laborious strength vested in his grip.

Then, there was the sound of something metallic sliding loose from a smooth place.

Followed by a peal of thunderous gunfire and panicked shrieks from the smooth-shaven dealer and St. Louis saloon pikers.

Ashley, snatched from the maelstrom of his killing rage by the heralding of gunfire, defensively reached for his revolver.

There was a ratcheting click. The sound every gambler and gunfighter knew. A double-action hammer drawn back in warning or finality.

Ashley, drawn erect in alarm, hand frozen for fear of what punishment drawing his pistol would bring, looked up to see Willow Sutliff's eyes glaring down a gun barrel at him. Confidence and surety, stiff as the December wind outside, whipped an unhappy smile on his brother's face. And through the lips came a tone colder than the spindles of ice dangling from every saloon house from here to the frozen Missouri River. "Daddy is asking you to come home. I, however, will not ask at all," he said. "Get up. Grab your shit. Let's go."

Under the sightline of his brother's gun, Ashley stepped away from the scattered mess of poker chips and the pummeled mess he had made of the other gambler. He walked past Will and patted him on the shoulder. "Forgive my previous tone. I was flush with my fever for the game." He turned back and gave his little brother his eyes, meanness melting from his smirk. "Right joyous am I to see your face."

"Sutliff," called the big gambler, who had found the grit to stand, clutching the shattered arm to his blood-soaked shirt. He screwed up his busted face and dared once more to make a threat. "I ever see you again, you're dead. You hear me? I'll unspool your guts in the goddamn street."

Ashley pushed through the doors and out into the cloudy, wind-tossed St. Louis night, giving the words no more mind than the weather outside.

The big man, unheard or ignored by Ashley, leveled his rage at Willow. "You best tell your brother to stay wherever he's going. St. Louis is no longer safe for him. Not a card house. Not an alleyway, day or night."

Will, saying nothing, shifted the sight of the gun to the wounded man.

The onlookers, seeing the relaxed clarity of Will's intent, stepped back to set distance between themselves and the potential cataclysm.

Only one of the big man's eyes widened, for the other was swelled shut. "Wait," he said, breathless, busted lips quivering, and the color of his anger drained out of him.

Will did wait for a moment, letting the lightning within him rage thunderless. Pistol aimed true, he considered. Arm steady, unwavering. And with a single flick of his wrist the revolver spun around, uncocked, and slid safely into the holster.

The dealer, placing his hands on his knees, let out a breath. "I swear to god, Walton, you gotta quit fuckin' calling people a cheat when you lose!"

Willow gave the saloon his back and made his way out into the street where his brother waited, hands stuffed into pockets of a black, threadbare summer coat, grinning up at the moon. This image of Ashley bathed in cloud-piercing moonbeams struck Will. For two years, Ashley's tumultuous leaving had erected within Will a great stockade of anger. Day over day, resentment had fortified that feeling. But to see him now, smirking at the sky as though he would challenge God at the great poker game of life, his brother's charm infiltrated that stockade with ease. And yet, all the happiness and love that welled up within Will at the sight made him all the more angry.

Unwilling to sock that stupid grin off his brother's face, he hit him with the truth outright. "Daddy's sick. Has been for weeks."

Ashley's eyes left the moon. The smirk left his face. "Sick with what?"

"Fever. Three doctors in the county, and none of them could help or identify his malady. Three days ago, he asked that I come find you. Bring you back home." Each successive word wilted his poise. "You know why."

Ashley looked at him, saying nothing.

"That's the whole of it."

Ashley swallowed hard. "How is mother?"

"Tough as an oak. At Daddy's side day and night. Aching for your return since the day you left." He began to walk along the thoroughfare, headed toward the river. "Momma takes care of Daddy. The two of us handle the hogs. We're thinking of getting into beef, too. Make a little extra."

The bricked streets of St. Louis, salted with snow, were lighted by towering streetlights and the burning white gas lamps of cardhouses and saloons. Horses carrying riders and pulling buggies clopped along the bricks, syncopating the heartbeat of what was, without question, the most arresting place Willow had ever been. "

"And Ellery?" asked Ashley, matching Will's stride.

"Taller than me now. Sprouted like you wouldn't believe." he said, catching sight of three tall factory smokestacks billowing black pillars toward the gray clouds above. "Big too. Like Uncle Chauncy. Where's your horse?"

Ashley shook his head, shrugging. "Died a few days back as the exclamation point on a month-long sentence of bad luck. I'd just managed to get on a run tonight when you stepped into that saloon. You come up the river, I guess?"

"Died a few days back," said Will, knowing an Ashley Sutliff lie even before the telling was through. "You know, I'm sure you can bluff with the best of them with cards, but it's never worked on me or Mother, or Daddy."

"Sold it three days ago when I ran out of money."

"You sold the gelding," said Will, entirely unsurprised. "To drink and gamble?"

"To survive, little brother."

Will threw out a dismissive gesture, rolling his fingers into the open air. "Daddy gave you that gelding."

"At Mother's behest."

"And against my protest."

Ashley laughed his unhappy laugh. "Yeah, Willow. He sure as shit did. Tell me, what makes you madder: the fact that I left or that Daddy ordered you to come get me?"

From not a long way off came the shrill cry of a steamboat disembarking from the frosty bank of the black Missouri River. It was perhaps the miracle of the decade that it had been a warmer winter than most, allowing steamers to carry freight and passengers to and from destinations that were blocked when the river froze hard and white as a block of marble. Will did not try to speak over the steamer's whistle but used its length to calm the lightning fury in his mind. When the shriek died, he made a bar of his arm and pressed it against his brother, stopping them both.

"I have never begrudged you for leaving," he said through gritted teeth, squaring his shoulders. He wanted to say more but found no words for that which he was feeling.

Ashley stared back, his eyes like embers ready to flare to life at the potential spark of an argument.

Will shook his head and let his hand fall away. "There's a steamboat headed toward home. It's a five-hour journey down river."

"I didn't forget where home is, Will. Why are you telling me—"

"Because I want you to know just how much time you have to figure out what you want to say to Daddy. If he's still alive. I advise you to brace yourself, big brother, because the sight of him will startle you. He is not as you remember him."

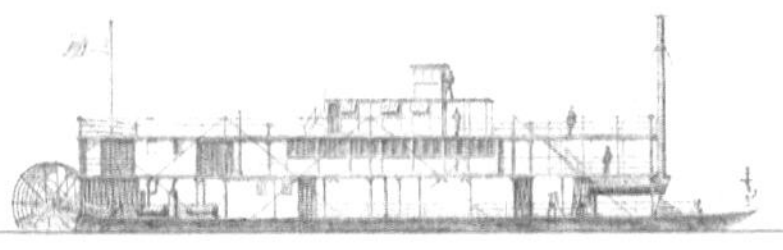

ABOARD THE STEAMER
MISSOURI TULIP,
MISSOURI RIVER

"I know that you're not likely to do me any favors, brother," said Ashley, surveying the sternwheel steamboat before them, "but my God, do not ask me to traverse the river in. . . in whatever the hell this is." The steamer, ringed in torch baskets lighting its form, was without question ten years older than any one of the other boats floating in the coal-black water.

"It's leaving soonest," Will said as he paid a sallow, grim-faced man in a button-down coat two dollars for deck passage, one bill for each man. "Time is more pressing to me than your comfort ever will be."

The old vessel, bathed in bright moonlight, was painted white with chipped blue lettering on the pilot house bearing its name: *Missouri*

Tulip. Ashley took a step onto the gray, weathered boarding plank, and it groaned. He stopped.

Will was watching him, shaking his head. "Will you come on?"

Ashley ignored him and turned to the attendant. "Was that the board or the boat?"

Will, frustrated, said, "Ashley."

"Can you attest to me right here and now," Ashley said to the attendant, "that this steamboat I am about to set foot upon will not sink with my added weight?"

The grim-faced man just stared at him, didn't respond.

"He can't say it," said Ashley. "This man does not believe in the integrity of the vessel. Why should I?"

"*Ashley.*"

"Sir," said the attendant in a tired and bored tone, "this is a one-hundred-fifty–ton steamboat vessel of the Flower Boat Packets Company. She has navigated the Mississippi and the junction where it meets the Missouri since long before today began, and she will continue to do so, by my estimation, until the end of time. If she sinks or her boilers explode and we all get thrown to damnation, you will have the pleasure of telling me and your companion I was wrong. Concurrently, if, by some strange and awful circumstance, you are knifed or shot or thrown overboard by one of the other passengers, say for running your smart-ass mouth or giving insult, Flower Boat Packets will not assume any responsibility for your death."

"See," said Ashley, giving the man a wink, "that's the kind of assurance I was looking for."

"Oh, happy day," said the attendant joylessly.

Ashley boarded, and he and Will walked the moonlit deck. The baseboards were made from slats of knotted pine, painted white as a church house and looking as old as the religion worshiped inside. Taking deck passage with the brothers Sutliff were freed Black laborers in threadbare coats and black-suited Creoles. Their standoffish demeanor clear, their occupations less so. A roost of tall blond dandies, speaking in a tongue Ashley did not know, escorted group of bonneted ladies all in blue dresses all looking past the steamer rail at the churning life and bustle of carriages and riders pouring among the city streets like blood pumping through a racing heart. High above the rail, near the simple wooden cube of the pilot house, a trio of frayed banners gently waved a premature goodbye to St. Louis. Faded gray and blue, trimmed in red, the tired flags seemed to long for earlier years or to be released from their station. Unclasped from their lofty place and folded one last time and put away, never again to know the wind. The attendant might have believed that this old tub would go on lasting, but Ashley could see she was close to the end of her service. High above it all, a cornflower moon threw its three-quarter radiance upon the whole of sleepy America, Missouri, the black river and the meager portion of passengers on the *Missouri Tulip*.

Ashley was fond of the night sky, taken by its ever-shifting sameness. In a way, it had become his teacher with its impenetrable depth, its winking charms. As a child he'd been enamored with the moon and the hazy stretch of the Milky Way reaching across a sky, salted with star upon star upon star. At the age of six, and likely before, his mind began to latch on to memories, and the stars in their courses had become his first friends. They always listened without rebuke. One cloudy night when he could not see those celestial boons, he had chased a streak of lightning, running from the tempest at home and into a thunderstorm that tried to claim his then thirteen years of life. Only a few years later, he had rode out on a white gelding toward the teaching moon and listening stars and all their clear, grand expanse, while his mother and brothers watched him from the porch and his father refused to come out of the house. No goodbyes had been spoken. His mother had hugged him as only mothers can, refusing to let go, no longer begging him to stay.

The whistle of the *Missouri Tulip* pierced the

air. Roustabouts wielding long wooden poles jabbed the sandy bank, shoving as a collective for all they were worth. The stern wheel rolled, dragging the steamer from the frost-rimed shore. When the *Tulip* came to the middle of the river there was another sharp scream from the whistle stack. A bell chimed twice, and the wheel reversed direction, churning south, its paddles chopping the face of the black waters to white.

Many of the passengers made their way up the warped wooden steps to seek out a seat or a drink at the bar on the meager texas deck. Ashley, wanting nothing to do with drink or the company of others, found an empty section of the main deck and leaned his elbows on a rail, scanning the shrinking city of St. Louis. The gay sounds of the city danced upon the moonlit waters, but the growing distance began to take them, then stole them entirely. A bend in the river soon thereafter removed the vision of the smokestacks, gaslighted streets, and the icy shoreline. Ashley promised himself that after his affairs were concluded at the hog farm and his familial responsibilities accomplished, he would not hesitate to come back to the city that had become home.

"It'll be here when you're done," said Will as he came to stand near Ashley. He did not lean upon the rail but stood tall and straight as a fence post.

"It's a marvelous place." Ashley dipped his gaze to the river, watching the ripples. "And I have grown very fond of it."

Will crossed his arms. "Why, Ashley, is that a loving sentiment I hear?"

He did not wish to engage in being poked fun at, so he raised the stakes of the conversation. "How is mother?"

"You already asked me that."

"I know. I believe 'aching for my return' is the way you twisted the knife."

"It's the unsubtle truth."

He lifted his head up to scan the riverbank, but clouds had rolled over the face of the moon so that little could be seen. "Tell me the whole of it, Willow."

"This is just like you," said Will, sniffing. "You don't wanna know how mother is. Daddy or Ellery either."

"But I do."

"You pretend at wanting to hear about mother's moods and feelings. Knowing you as only a brother can, I imagine after two years of not writing or visiting, your selfish mind has not wondered if we were *okay* but if we still talk about you. If we still miss you. If, each and every night, our four minds come together and as one collective passel of mourners we say, 'I wish Ashley had never left.'" Will shook his head as if disbelieving the truth he was telling. "You have always been self-absorbed. Thinking little of others. And in this way you have become the worse kind of selfish wretch, seeing everyone else as cards in a hand you've been dealt, rather than other players at the table."

"Oh, how you have longed to say that to me," said Ashley. "Knowing *you* as only I can, you've been tailoring that response for months at least. Maybe since the night I left." He turned, throwing his appraisal toward fence-post-straight Willow. "I did not leave the hog farm because I am selfish—though I am, I openly admit. Our father cut a section of the world for himself at my age, found a woman worth putting up with, fought against the rebs, and helped kill slavery in the country that provided him the opportunity to do it all. And you think me selfish because I wanted the same chance? I left because I could not imagine the course of my life being staked to such a poor, uneventful landscape. There was no living to be done at the farm."

A small thing, a little sway, rolled through Will. The crease of his jaw bulged, and pain filled his eyes. "There was us," he said.

Slashed to the soul by truth in his brother's words and wanting nothing more to do with the feeling, Ashley angrily pushed himself away from the rail. "I'm thirsty."

Ashley turned and walked toward the texas deck, toward the bustling strangers inside at the bar. Perhaps someone had struck up a poker game.

Willow let him go. Refusing to look back as he listened to his brother's silver spurs jingle along the wooden planks and ring up the steps and through the doors of the texas deck. Forked bolts of anger blistered through him, striking the center of his heart. *So goddamn selfish.* The thought boomed over and over, annihilating all others. He hated both the shock of this feeling and, perhaps more so, that it was within his brother's power to conjure the storm.

Looking out into the flat darkness, Will saw nothing. Heard nothing. His wild anger, contained within the thunderhead of his mind, assailed all his senses until finally, in a hushed whisper he hissed, "So selfish."

He thought of Ellery, and of how the three-man job of the farm's upkeep had been left to his little brother alone. The mending of fences, the feeding and watering and sheltering and grooming of the stock, and the everyday challenges that came bright and early as the sun. A mare had run off two days ago and, because Will had been sent to fetch Ashley, she was likely gone for good. A seventy-five–dollar horse lost, all for the sake of a man who cared nothing for the price of the mare or the cost of his actions. He thought of his mother who, though the evening grew long, was likely sitting in the wavering lamplight of her bedroom, lightly dabbing the sweat from his father's fevered brow.

So goddamn *selfish*, he thought.

Shaking his head, Will tried to calm himself, taking slow, steady breaths that were the wind rolling the storm clouds beyond the landscape of himself. It was a landscape he saw clearly in his mind's eye: a long, golden plain of little hills, empty of anything but the brightness of the sun and the short grass shining bright as wheat ready for threshing. These were Willow's fields of gold where he could see the distance of things, the vision of what such a landscape might become if watched closely. What he might make himself into. What he could become.

Ashley had been the first-born, given everything. But all the man wanted to do was drink and gamble, running from responsibilities that were his birthright. 'The hog farm' he had called it repeatedly, a sour tone each time. That's all Ashley could see, the muddy ground and the trundling stock, refusing the work that came with them. Will didn't know what the landscape within Ashley looked like, but for himself it was a dream that had begun with his mother and father and which he, as their son, would keep alive and nurture into prosperity. Breathe the breath of his life into it. Make it his own.

For the remaining three hours of the steamboat's southeastward journey toward Nedemore, Will pulled little cigars out of his breast pocket one at a time, smoking one after the other until his tongue was raw. There were moments when he would squint through the cigar smoke to wonder at the rippling black of the river and the moonlighted thicket running wild and white along Missouri bank. No fewer than a dozen times he looked back at the texas deck to see if his brother would come sauntering back down the steps. Return to him. After the fourth or fifth glance, Will's quiet yearning for his brother's company, which he would never admit to, became the old, familiar anger. And by the twelfth time, the longing was the furthest from his mind. The thunderclouds had rolled over the hills of his heart, their gold grass shadowed to the gray of iron.

So selfish, he thought.

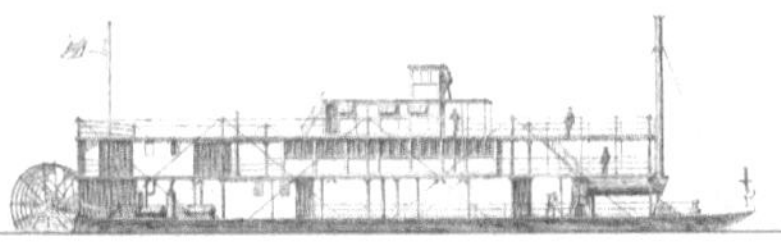

CHAPTER THREE

Near La Fourche à Duclos, Ste. Genevieve County, Missouri

The *Missouri Tulip* pulled into a little wood yard where gnarled pine and cottonwood cylinders were stacked in long rows four times higher than a man. She blew her whistle, letting God and Ashley Sutliff and the river and the land, powdered white as a Sunday pastry, know her ancient bulk had arrived.

The brothers Sutliff disembarked with neither of them saying anything to the other. Ashley, his spirit lifted by whiskey and the shy mirth of the women in blue dresses, who had turned out to be Mennonites or methodists or some damn such or other, walked just behind Will. The grim attendant who Ashley had traded barbs with stood at the walking plank, watching them pass by.

"I suppose you were right about this steamer's capability," Ashley said.

The attendant only shook his head. It was clear by the look in his eyes that while he had likely never been a happy man, he was closer to being one by Ashley's leaving.

A muddy road, cut to pieces by foot traffic and brown as a chocolate cake, curved around the copse of cottonwoods and pines, which numbered too many to be a thicket, too few to make a forest. They would soon be cut down in service of the steamers heading south, where the black Missouri met the muddy waters of the Mississippi. The landing was known as Les Pauvres l' atterrissage, the Poor Landing, among the locals. The Poor was a place Ashley had come several times as a boy, and not much had changed since he had seen it last two years prior. Aside from the gray, wooden office used for the selling of wood, there was a single general store with a post office inside and, just behind it, a weather-beaten livery stable.

Will crunched through the soft snow and into the store. Ashley did not follow but took in all the quiet that the loud braying of St. Louis had made him forget. What for the creaking hinge of the general store door and thud of it shutting, there was little other sound, everything still. So still that he could hear his every breath and feel the beating of his heart. The whiskey had given him warmth and poured itself over the frustrations with Will and his anxieties about where he was going. Had made him downright agreeable, he thought, allowed him to forget the purpose of the journey and the city where his heart ached to return.

He heard his brother's voice and another he didn't know coming from behind the ramshackle store. To lift a bit of the mistiness from his thoughts, he rolled a cigarette. Cupping his hands in front of the cylinder, he struck the tobacco to life. The smoke filled his lungs, and clarity flowered in his mind.

The sound of shodden hooves came toward him. Looking up from hands giving alms to the drifting smoke, he saw his brother astride a black gelding. Its velvet sheen and braided gray mane were unmistakable. The gelding's name was Martin, he was fourteen years old, and from colt to stud to tempered mount, he had ferried but one rider, and it was not the man riding him today. Ashley's boozy fine feeling melted like snow in the late morning sun. The cigarette soured, losing all its potency.

Willow must have seen the look on Ashley's face, for he grinned, watching the wound open. Martin chuffed and shook his head, and the way his long lips curled, he looked as though he were grinning too. And when Ashley saw the black saddle ringed in polished steel from horn to concho, from rigging to billet strap to tie-down, the wound opened wider.

"Let you borrow his horse *and* saddle," said Ashley, trying to make the big hurt small.

Will shook his head. "Not borrow. Gave," he said. "Long before he was sick. Not long after you left."

Ashley grinned, lying all the way. "Good for you, little brother."

"Climb up here with me," said Will, offering his hand.

"Believe I'll walk."

Will glared, his arm unmoving. "Don't be prideful."

Ashley looked away from his brother's hand toward the general store. "Maybe they've got a horse I can—well, I can't buy it, but I'll bet they'll let me borrow it."

"Brother," said Will, soft and suddenly tender.

Ashley turned back to him.

"Daddy asked me to come get you to say goodbye. Please do not cause his final request of me to prove a failure." His eyes wetted and his jaw clenched. "Please."

In youth, Ashley had rarely seen his brother this way, but the starkness of the sight had, each and every time, made clear the desperate desire to please living inside Will. And so, tired of both taking and giving emotional wounds on their short trip, Ashley took Will by the hand and squeezing tightly and holding fast, let his brother's strength carry him up.

"Hold on to me," said Will.

Ashley wrapped his arms around his little brother's waist and, with a little pat to signal he was ready to go, felt Martin's wild power all so quickly become speed.

The cold wind cut hard against Willow Sutliff's face, but it could not blow the smile from his lips.

"That's it. Come, on!" hollered Will, feeling his brother's arms tighten around him. It was a strange sensation, feeling his brother clinging to him just as Will had done to Ashley in boyhood, driven into older brother's room by nightmares or the excited want to share the hearing of bull-frog songs.

Martin set unto his purpose of making war with time, his only competitor. He'd been gelded a year back, proving too dangerous for the ranch mares with his roughness and biting nature. "Horses live to breed and run, son," Will's father had said many years ago. "And for the gelded, the desire to breed may wane, but the love of the race stays with them until their heart can take no more." And so, Martin's singular joy to run always proved their father true. Freshly fed and watered and lathered in his prime, he raced along the road. With a long, prideful gait he chewed up the doughy mud, carrying the brothers Sutliff on the road home with a desire, Will believed, to get back to the place where he belonged. A yearning shared between home-bound traveler and the horse willing to take him there.

The road straightened. Trees crowded closer. And the rich light pierced every inch of frost all over the Missouri splendor, setting the foliage to shine as if encrusted by millions diamonds in the mid-morning sun. The chill of his homeland rolled over Will, freezing the anxiety within him. He loved to ride. Loved the land where he'd grown up riding even more. It was this act, living in its simplicity, that made him capable of forgetting about sickness and pain and the death awaiting every living man.

They came a fork in the road that curved toward a little creek, and slowed to cross where the clear water shallowed, running quietly over stones older than every name given to the land by Man. Chopping up the waters, Martin lost little time and shifted into a gallop again. And through a spray of grass more stubborn than winter, whose center had long been worn out by footfalls and riders and wagons, the gelding rushed. Harder and faster. Martin's ribs shoved against Will's legs then constricted, blowing wind from his titanic lungs so hot that the steam of his breath could be seen. Long the three sped over the white ground toward the Sutliff acreage where they could see the hogs and the cattle roaming not too far from the house where the brothers had been born.

After not too much further, Will eased up on Martin, pulling the still eager gelding to slow. The house sat before them upon one of the few hills of the otherwise flat land. The dark wood of the ranch-house facade and the gray smoke billowing from its trio of chimneys set their shadow against Will. The joy of running to get home was over, and now the uncertainty of what was waiting inside rolled the storm clouds back over his mind.

"Well," said Ashley, "there it is. Just like I left it."

Willow did not respond, hating the matter-of-fact, dismissive tone his brother employed.

In the distance, not too far from the northern reach of the property where a great ring of cottonwoods began, Willow saw a figure among mounded snow, digging into the ground with a shovel. "Ellery," he said and pointed.

It was then Ashley's turn to look, to understand what the youngest of them was doing.

Are we too late, thought Willow, despairing. *Is Daddy already gone?*

Will brought them near the wrap-around porch. He halted Martin and felt Ashley slide off the horse. And then the front door opened, and a woman he didn't know walked out of the house. She was round, with brown hair that ran in tangled whisps about her spectacles and ample face. Pulling the brown skirts of her dress clear of the frame, she closed the front door gently.

"Ashley. Willow," she said, walking down the steps of the porch toward them, "your father is living, though for how much longer only the Lord can say. Your mother is inside, making coffee."

Martin shook his head, wanting to run again.

Willow stared at the woman, uncertain as what to say.

"Pardon me, ma'am," said Ashley, "but who the hell are you?"

CHAPTER FOUR

SUTLIFF ACREAGE
STE. GENEVIEVE COUNTY, MISSOURI

"You are not pardoned, Ashley Sutliff," the woman said. Her head tipped forward like a bowl, and her pale blue eyes bulged in offense. Her fingers released the wool of her skirts, then wrapped themselves around a thick, dark belt around her waist. And she went to say something else, as if she were going to lambaste him with rebuke. But she tilted back, standing straight once again. "I suppose you were young the last time I was here. Too young to remember. Listen, I'm Carolina Ellison, a friend of your parents for many years" she said. Almost all the quick tension he had seen seemed to relax, and her lips furrowed into a sad smile. "Your mother wants to see you inside."

"That's where we were hurrying to get to," said Will. He slid out of the saddle, his boots crunching in the heel-deep snow.

"Just him." She looked from Will back to Ashley. "She wants to see you alone."

Ashley turned to Will, frowning.

Willow wrinkled his mouth to one side and shook his head, saying only, "Of course she does."

"Ellery needs help," said Carolina. "That's what she told me to tell you."

"I'll hurry and come help, too," said Ashley so quickly and so earnestly that it surprised him.

It must have surprised Will as well, because for the first time since his younger brother had walked into the saloon there seemed to be respect in his eyes. Maybe even appreciation.

"Lemme help you with Martin," the woman said to Will. Approaching the gelding, she lifted a hand and placed it on his frost-rimed nose. Martin leaned into her touch. "You remember your Auntie Carolina, don't you, sugar."

For the life of him, Ashley could not remember this woman, and though he had met several Carolinas in his life, none of them had been her. None had been that big or had near the amount of grit in their tone. Come to think of it, all the Carolinas in his life had been either whores or dancing girls, which made him wonder if Carolina had even been their real names.

Without asking, she took Martin's reins into her hand, placed the other on Will's lower back, and began to walk them toward the barn. "You really don't remember me?" She smiled at him.

Ashley didn't hear his brother's answer over the slash of wind that blew across his already wind-burned cheeks. He realized that he was standing at the front porch alone, in the cold. Riding that long and that hard had also put a pain in his hips and thighs. He hadn't ridden like that in, well, he couldn't remember. And he thought about that for a time, that and St. Louis and the saloons, and the women waiting for his company and his money, and the table games and the chips, and all of the things that were not the front door of the place he had grown up.

Ashley sucked his teeth and looked out toward the southern edge of the acreage, where the sloppy hog pens lay quiet and empty, still gated in timbers he had cut from the west thicket at the age of thirteen. The gate was open, but for all his effort to listen he heard none of the hungry grunting and squealing and piercing racket that haunted the low places within himself. The places where he sheltered the hidden shame of being nothing more and never becoming something greater than the son of a harvester of pigs. But the sky was blue, and the gleam of the snow piled over the hog house, the timber fence, the mud, and the whole reach of the land made him remember another feeling. The simple stillness that steadies the disquiet in the busy mind. The overwhelming power of memories and the inexhaustible fire to remember them, even when they were sometimes all he wanted to forget. In the empty hog pens walked the living ghosts of his childhood, and when looking there he saw the spectral image of his father, tall, lean, working hard as a mule before the sun found its way above the trees.

Behind him, the sound of the front door opening filled the quiet air, and in knowing who would be there, he found that he could not turn to face her. A part of him wanted the woman who had birthed him into this world to see the adult cut of him, to see the man he had become even in the two long years since he had ridden away from this place on that lonesome October night.

And so he stood there looking out at the whited land and the blue of the now cloudless sky, waiting. Waiting to hear—

"Son."

The word leveled all the rocky terrain that comprised their history.

And suddenly caring very little about how

she would see him, only that she would see him at all, he turned to look at her.

Though she appeared frailer and more tired, diminished in a way that put a deep regret within him, it was the unmistakable color of her smiling eyes that made an Easter of the snowy world around them. And all his very grown-up cares and hopes and dreams of wanting to be more than who he thought living here would make him become, Ashley stepped toward her. His lip trembled, and he called her by the name that only he as the first-born could have uttered first into the world, changing the both of them.

"Mother," he said.

His mother—the creator of three boys and every inch of every little happiness those children had experienced across the landscape of their years—lifted her fingertips to her lips. Her eyes caught the light, pooling with tears. For a moment she looked angry, shaking her head, but then she once again became the woman who could never be angry at all. Not with him.

Ashley wanted to pull his mother's tired frame into his arms, to share his young, inexhaustible stamina and tell her it would be alright. To promise that he would do whatever he must to make *her* alright. But his arms did not lift, and he made no promises. For as much as his mother owned his heart, St. Louis was in his soul.

It was as if she could see it, the little battle playing over in his mind. And in her eyes was the burning hope that her child had not returned simply for one last goodbye. The wish, as all mothers must wish in some way, her children will crave the nearness of home more powerfully than they feel the draw of the world.

Unable to stoke the fires of hope, he did not go to her, did not wrap his arms around that venerable matriarch and say a single apology for all he had put her through.

It would become the second greatest regret of his life.

"You're home," she said, rolling her shoulders back to bring herself up to full height. "Good. Now, come inside. Your father is waiting on you."

They went inside.

The house smelled of coffee and well-worn wood that creaked and groaned, all as it had in the time before.

"Take your boots off," she said, making her way down the long foyer. "I know how they treat the floors in those St. Louis gin palaces. I will not have mud all over my—" She stopped short upon realizing Ashley had already sat down on the little pine bench to remove that which he knew was not allowed in the house. "I know, mother," he said. "I remember."

"Did you say hello to Ellery?" she asked.

“No, ma’am.” He finally got one boot off, the mud on the heel thick as putty on his palm. “We’d just rode up when— Speaking of hellos, who was that woman who just left?”

“That’s my friend Carolina Ellison. Guessing you don’t remember her.”

“Should I?” He slid off his other boot and stood there, snow white socks on the cream runner carpet loomed with blooming bluebells, ivy, and dandelions.

“If I had a nickel for all the things you’ve forgotten, son—”

“You’d be a millionaire,” he said and smiled at her, remembering that too.

She pursed her lips, trying to control her expression, but the smile came through anyway. Then she turned again, leading him into the kitchen.

The nearly immaculate floors bore but one major scar: a three-inch-long white line near a quarter inch deep from the day they’d purchased the potbelly stove. He’d been helping his father carry it when Ashley dropped his end, marking the wood for all time. The stove had looked so new then, the dull iron somehow finding a way to shine. Now, he saw the little splinters of wood around the claw feet, blackened edges on the wood hatch, and smears of grease on the flat top where the percolator stood. His mother went over to the stove and drew a cup from the hanging hooks. She poured coffee, her back still facing him. "Coffee?"

"No, ma'am," he said.

"Willow told you all of it, I assume. That only heaven can mend what the doctors failed to understand." She put the percolator down but didn't turn.

Ashley looked at the four empty chairs surrounding the post oak pedestal table. Four chairs where there had once been five. "He told me."

His mother stepped over to the table, carrying the blue tin mug in both hands. "Will you sit with me a while?"

"Yes, ma'am."

She reached into a pocket of her simple dress and drew out a cigarette. Every morning, she rolled three, he knew, and he was glad to see that while so many things had changed, this had remained. She had always said that for every boy she'd birthed, she deserved equal reprieve. She leaned one elbow onto the table, held the cigarette between two fingers, and waited on him.

Ashley produced a match from his pocket, and flared it to life.

His mother took a long, hard drag and sighed. The smoke swirled from her lips. And she looked at him with eyes the shade of river valley waters and of the evergreens imperfectly mirrored in their flow. They carried within their color more memories of Ashley than Ashley had of himself. "I have missed you, son," she said. "So very much."

Unable to meet her gaze, he examined every inch of the dinner table's grain. "I know, mother. I missed you too."

"Your daddy is in there." She pointed to their bedroom. "Been there for weeks. He got sick a little before that. Will probably told you all about it on y'all's way here."

"He didn't."

"He didn't say, or you didn't think to ask?"

"I asked," he said, unable to recall if he had.

She let out a little laugh. "I know my boys. Willow Sutliff would have told you, that's his way. It's your way not to ask."

"I'm here," he said. He didn't like being poked or scolded, and the notion that she would choose to do so at this moment frustrated him. "I could have chose not to."

"No, you couldn't."

"You don't know all of me, mother."

"Ashley," she said. "Look at me, son."

Unable to refuse her, even in frustration, he obeyed.

"I know my boys. And if you had told your brother that you were unwilling to come then. . ." She laughed again, a low, tired sound. "I believe he might have shot you."

Though he fought against it, he smiled.

"See?" she asked, though it wasn't a question.

Ashley's smile slouched. "How did Daddy get sick?"

She flicked the ash of her cigarette into a little ashtray at the center of the table. "Don't have any idea at that. But you know what he's like. He tried to ignore it while continuing to work. Then, when it got worse, he tried to work through it, believing he was stronger than whatever it was. Eventually, he couldn't work at all. The fever showed up, and now. . ." Her voice broke, and all the spring seasons within her fell away. She pulled hard on the cigarette, the little white cylinder trembling with her lips. "Now we know his destination. I don't know when it'll be, but I know it'll be soon." The smoke did nothing to hide her tears. "Much, much sooner than I ever thought it would be."

Ashley put a hand over hers. "It's not your fault, mother. You know how stubborn he is. Hell, it's where all three of us get it."

"No," she said suddenly, as if offended. "You will not blame your daddy for your faults. I will not allow it, Ashley. You are impatient. Brooding and moody. Your wild tumper, sure, that one I will allow your father to claim. But the rest you got from me." Her voice was sterner than he could ever remember. Cold as it had ever been.

She took another long drag from her waning cigarette, blew the smoke from the corner of her mouth. "You've only ever known me as your mother, son. You never knew me in the way I was before. And I do not blame you for not knowing. How could you, boy growing into a man and a brother twice over, know the slightest bit about what a girl's life with no one but a wicked father was like? What kind of woman it produced."

She drew her hand away from his. "Your desire to run off, be something, that belonged to me once, too. My father, the men around me, all of them told me that I had to be a particular way. Had to bend at a social angle my mental shape could never allow. And so I ran from them and lived frontier life." Her gaze became distant, slowly drifting away from him to lean their full weight on the room where his father now lay. "And then I found *him*. A man who never asked me to bend. Who always said, "Leigh, you can be who you are. Whoever you want to be. So long as you'll be it with me."

Fresh tears fell from her green eyes like dew curling from morning grass. "And I was, Ashley. I was a different woman entirely. Living a life not unlike your St. Louis dream. All of it with him. He never tried to make me anything other than his; whatever shape I leaned into, your daddy would find a way to hold it. Keep me upright."

"I didn't mean to say he was to blame—"

She shook her head, cutting him off. "Yes. You did. And I will not have it. Not here in the house we built, and never not once after he's in the ground. He's more than your daddy, more than my husband, more than a man who fought for human dignity wherever he saw the battleground reveal itself. Those things were a part of him, but they were not all he was. They were his stations, his posts. The choices he made. Such a small portion of his heart and his generous, dedicated soul."

"I know, Mother," he said. "I know."

"Oh my boy," she said, reaching out to touch him softly on the cheek, as if she were smoothing the wrinkles life had yet to bestow. A gesture as young as the child still inside him and as old as mothers and sons. "You don't know a goddamn thing." She smiled. "But I am hopeful you will. You don't even realize, son. You broke your father's heart when you left. And when you broke that man's heart, your broke your momma's too."

And with those words, a continent of years fractured inside him.

"Mother, I—" But he found himself incapable of explaining. The mass of the man, sinking into an invisible, churning gulf, said simply, "I came back for us to have our goodbyes."

There was a little sound that left her lips,

pity in the smoke. "Have your goodbyes? Have your *goodbyes*? There is so much the world is yet to teach you, but as your youth becomes age, you will learn. Saying goodbye is a greater event than to simply carry a body to its resting place. Goodbye is a feeling that stays with you forever. Walks beside you when you are alone and until fully alone, when goodbyes are said to you, ferries you into what comes after goodbye."

Silence fell over them, his mother nodding slowly.

"That education starts now, my love," she said. "Go to him. Whatever love for him you left behind when you rode off from home, pick it up again. Carry it with you."

Ashley stood up and walked from the open kitchen to his parent's bedroom door.

The grain of the cedar door caught the cold afternoon sun so that it shone like summertime honeycomb. A black iron knob set within the blond wood waited, and though he knew the knob would be easy to turn, the weight of what waited within unmanned him. From some lonely, forgotten field of his childhood, a child's fear peeped through the tall grass of memory and gazed at him. Those eyes were his own, young and wild, compelling him to pause. Ashley gazed back, looking at who he had once been, confronting the dreaded knowledge that going through this door would be a single step crossing into an unknown territory of life.

"Ashley," his mother said softly. Still sitting, still smoking. "Go on, honey. Waiting gives the devil time."

As if drawn away by her voice, the young eyes within the field of Ashley's memory darted back into the high growth. The blades of tall grass swished, then steadied. Closing his eyes, he took a deep breath and opened the door, and himself, to what was waiting inside.

The room was as it had always been, though it seemed so small now. Incapable of holding the full harvest of his youth. A low fire burned in the ash-laden hearth. Though he was vaguely aware of the oak duo of wardrobes, the pine chest of drawers, and his mother's stationary desk, for Ashley there was only the post oak bed and the curl of a man beneath buffalo blankets.

Captain Forrest M. Sutliff, a titan personality reaching higher than taller men but whose physical height never reached six feet, lay unmoving, facing away from him. Ashley watched, heart in his throat, to see if his father's shoulders would rise and fall. The aching inside him honed his vision. He wondered what to say. . . how to know if anything would be heard.

But his father's shoulders seemed still. And the only breathing Ashley heard was his own.

And then, from the field of grass within him,

a desperate sound flowed out of Ashley. "Daddy," he said, breaking the silence. The man speaking a boy's word.

His father's shoulders rose, crested as a wave, then sagged again.

Never once in the span of his nineteen years had Ashley called in such a way only to receive no answer. He circled the bed, his heavy footfalls overtaking easily the soft crackle of the fire and the hushed breathing of the dwindling patriarch.

Stepping closer, Ashley became aware of all the time he would not have. The words that would go unspoken from henceforth. For though there had been few years of joy between Ashley and his father, he would ache for more of the less happy years. To gaze upon the harsh Irish disapproval in his father's brown eyes, rather than to see them open no more. Hear the scolding impatience and listen to opinions Ashley would never share.

His father, a bent, diminished icon of all that Ashley had once hoped to grow into, did not stir. Did not answer.

"Daddy," he said again, this time pleading.

The man grimaced, shifted only a little.

Then, slowly and with great effort, his father opened his eyes. He searched through some unseen mist between him and his son. "Willow?"

Ashley grit his teeth but kept quiet. How it stung to be misnamed.

"No. . ." said his father, wholly possessed by exhaustion. The corners of his mouth, flecked with dried spittle, lifted into a smile that was unfamiliar to Ashley.

"Ashley." The word was long, more sigh than proclamation.

To hear his name on his father's lips, the recognition and the surety, spread an invisible salve over the sting of being misidentified. "Yes, sir," said Ashley, for it was all he could think to say.

His father tried to roll onto his back, but the struggle was too great. The veteran strength of his years, left in the forge of sundering fever for weeks, had become brittle. "You came home. I did not think you would."

"I'm here," said Ashley. "I'm right here."

"You are," his father began, voice straining, withered beyond his forty-seven years. But strength came back into it at the end. "Only for a piece. Only for a time."

It was a phrase he had used for as long as Ashley could remember. It came to him in that moment: he had never heard his father say a goodbye. Ashley had never kenned the phrase's full meaning and purpose until now.

Only for a piece of my life will I be without you and you without me. Only for a time will we be apart.

"It is happiness itself to see you," said his father. "How. . . how does it feel to be home?"

Ashley kneeled down, setting their eyes at equal level. He answered honestly. "I am not sorry that I left," he said, tears pooling at the corners of his eyes, "but I am sorry I was gone."

Sweat beaded the sick man's brow. He blinked heavily, his eyes staying closed so long that for a moment Ashley thought he had fallen asleep.

Ashley reached into his coat and produced a frayed silk handkerchief. Folding it once over, he placed it atop his father's head.

Though he did not open his eyes, his father spoke. "Carolina. . . Is she still here?"

"Yes, sir." Ashley gently dabbed the brow dry.

"She came looking for my help, only to find me diminished. Our family owes her and her brother a great deal. Years ago, a promise was made. A pact. And so, our acreage at the cost of a favor. But I am unable to fulfill that promise. So, I sent Willow to find you."

Of course, thought Ashley, *this could not be about me or us. Even at the end, it is about you.* But he did not say it. His mother's request to carry again all the love he had left behind rested itself on him. "Me? Why not send one of your favorite dutiful sons?"

His father breathed deep, sank deeper into the

horsehair pillows. Tired. Sweat rolled from a hairline the color of old wood and iron. "A father has no favorites. And duty is a requirement of all sons. Ellery is too young. Willow has little of the bend from which he gets his namesake. This leaves you, Ashley. My strong son, from whom I have learned so much about other men as you became one. There so much of your mother inside you; her strength, her stubbornness. I only wish…" He breathed deep again. And again, quicker. "I am sorry that neither you or I grew into the person the other hoped they would become. I need you to do this thing. Not because we owe, but because we promised."

The sweat continued to roll down his father's face, but Ashley did not lift the handkerchief again, for it was wadded in the tight fist he'd made. A clenched ball hidden from his father's sight.

"It will be dangerous, son," he said. "That I promise you. But of all the boys, neither danger nor the fear it wields has never slowed you." He drew out a hand from beneath the bedsheet, fingers shaking from the effort, and placed it on Ashley's shoulder. The single limb seemed to bear the full weight of the man. "I remember a boy who, angry with me for making him cut winter firewood on a summer day, waited until nightfall and ran headlong into a thunderstorm. Into the lightning and the spray and the darkness surrounding it all."

"I remember, too." Which was true to say, but less true than Ashley made it sound.

"I am sure you do. A great act of defiance for you. And what I saw was a great act of *independence*. I witnessed you deciding what kind of man you were going to be. And that's exactly the kind of man, the kind of son, I am proud to send to repay this debt."

"And if I say no?" asked Ashley, a gambler wanting to know the stakes.

"A broken promise. A little toll for Ashley Sutliff. At the cost of my word, which has meant everything to me."

Ashley then asked the question he had truly wanted to ask. "And if I say yes?"

"What do you mean?"

"What will it mean to you if I say yes."

He shook his head, as if unable to understand.

"What will it mean to you if I agree, Daddy?"

There was a winnowing of his father's face, as if the words had blown dark clouds over him, diminishing him further. "You are asking me if I will love you better."

Ashley grit his teeth. "I am."

"It is an impossibility," he said, his voice so tired, so strained. "From babe to child to man. . ." The hand resting on Ashley's shoulder squeezed, finding its old power for a piece of that moment and for the briefest of time. "There is no more of me to give. You have it all. Always will."

Willow had said little while walking toward the stable, though Carolina tried to coax words from him with her conversation with Martin.

"Look at how big you got," she'd said. "Yes, you grew-up just fine. Strong and tall and proud."

But he said nothing, knowing her intent. The whole of his mind was focused on the north portion of the acreage. Not too far off, Ellery was standing in the waist-deep pit with the shovel, plunging and tossing clumps of wet, black earth into a pile. The sound of his work became the only thing Will could hear.

"Looks like he could use some help," said Carolina. "Doesn't he, Martin?"

The gelding shook his head so that the steel rings of his tack jingled like mirthless Christmas bells in the cold winter air.

Will picked up a spade hanging just inside the stable, set it against his shoulder, and nestling the shaft in the crook of his elbow, crunched through the snow toward his brother. It was a long short trip, his feet taking their time. His mind preoccupied with the journey ahead.

"Heyo," Will said.

Ellery's spade drove into the ground with a

heavy, wet crunch, scraped against little stones, and sent another mound of mud flying out of the hole. The youngest of the three brothers was about his business. Focused. Likely hearing nothing but the sound of the spade and all the inches of progress that came one scoop at a time.

Will came to the edge of the hole that was wide enough for two coffins but not yet deep enough for a proper burial. "Need some help?"

Ellery jammed the spade into the ground, blew out a breath, and flung a pile of earth over his shoulder. "It's lonely work. But I figure your task to St. Louis was lonely too," he answered without answering. Clutching the shaft so that it supported his weight, Ellery dabbed his brow against the arm of his red flannel shirt made maroon with sweat. "You find him?"

"Sure did."

"He come with you?"

Will sat down, letting his legs dangle over the edge of the hole. "He's inside with Mother and Daddy now."

Ellery, brown-eyed and handsome and jacketed in brawn, smiled a smile that, like the rest of his build, was the envy of all the men who met him. "Looks like you owe me ten dollars."

"He took convincing."

"That was not the bet, Willow."

"At gunpoint."

Ellery shook his head. His smile grew. "Either

by threat of knife or gun or cannon fire, makes no difference. He came."

Will crooked his head toward the spade over his shoulder. "Do you want some help?"

Ellery surveyed his work, estimating. "I'm not tired. Shouldn't take me too much longer."

"You dug too wide, you know."

"I've never made a grave before."

"I have." Will slid into the hole, approaching his brother. "Years ago, though."

"With the preacher's wife?"

And they leaned into each other, without word, and embraced as they always did in a brotherly hug punctuated by a two hard pats on the back. Then, they drew back.

"Jessica Goodwin. Ten years now. I still remember her name and, luckily for you, Daddy's instruction on the width and depth needed for the hole. Now, you stand against that end," he said, pointing east. "And I'll stand here. We dig until it's over my head and eye level with you."

"Aren't you worried you won't be able to climb out?"

The joke caught Will all wrong. A vision passed over his mind, the terrible imagining of his arms failing to pull humself out of the burial plot, too weak to support his weight. The snow-wetted edge too slick for his fingers to find purchase. He shoved that thought down to the secret place, wherever it is that people hide sudden irrational fears. "Very funny."

Ellery set his back against the east wall, lifted the spade and thrust it into the ground like a conqueror making his claim. All the while, smiling at his older brother, a smug winner.

Will took off his coat and set it on the lip of the hole. And rolling up his sleeves and changing the subject of the loathsome requirement of digging their father's grave together, said to his brother, "Ten dollars."

"You might be older," said Ellery, "but there's a lesson I understood very early that you've refused to learn."

"That being?"

"Never bet against Ashley."

Willow sank his spade into the ground and labored with his brother until the work was done.

PART TWO

To Carry a Body
to its Resting Place

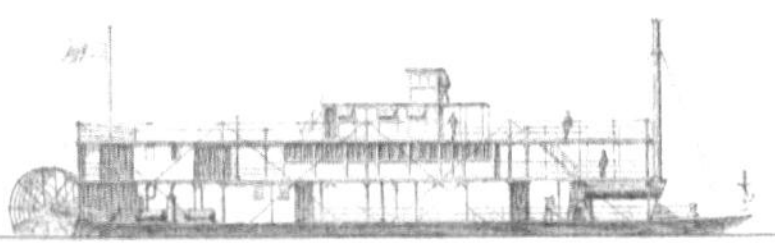

CHAPTER FIVE

SUTLIFF ACREAGE
STE. GENEVIEVE COUNTY, MISSOURI

The brothers Sutliff, all three, were sitting in the oil lamp glow of the parlor when their mother walked into the room, her face the definitive portrait of strength. It was near midnight. Ellery had been reading. Ashley had been mindlessly shuffling a deck of cards, watching Willow watching the clock. And when she came in, they all, to a man, stood up.

"He's gone, boys," she said. "I held him as he went."

Ellery looked to the ground.

Willow looked away.

Ashley looked at his mother, overwhelmed with admiration. There was an easement of pressure on her, relief in the way her anxiety smoothed now to sorrow. And he watched her even more keenly than he had been watching Willow, and he saw the way she looked to Ellery then to Willow and finally to Ashley. None of his brothers saw it but him, the power of the woman standing resolute in the face of death. It was a gift. And more, it was a lesson Ashley would practice matching for the rest of his days. One he would never master in the way his mother did in that moment.

Ellery set his book on the couch and went to his mother, never meeting her eye. He wrapped the whole of his great big self around her, and his shoulders began to shake. He quietly sobbed as the gravity of the world he knew became too great for his young, Atlas-like strength.

"I know, honey," she said. "I know."

Willow gazed into some far-off place set on a lamp-lighted horizon within the pine knots of the slatted ceiling, unknowable to everyone but him. Ashley wanted to go to him, to place a comforting hand on his shoulder and find a way to say, "It's okay, little brother. I am here."

Wasn't that the job of the eldest? To reassure. To bind together the siblings with the soft, strong bonds of understanding. Yes, of course. It was his father's chiefest message. The requirement of his first-born son, spoken since the boy could walk and work and remember. It saddled his wild heart for a moment, and he felt shame, because being saddled by such a requirement made him want to run again. Head back to St. Louis, leaving all requirements behind.

And so, finding a middle ground within himself, Ashley did not run for St. Louis and did not step to comfort his brother. He stood there. Still. Watching the devastation roll over the Sutliff family, each of them taking it in their own way.

Ellery kissed his mother and then turned and without hesitation pulled Willow over to him into a hug. Will's face showed his surprise, suddenly drawn out of the horizon line of the pine ceiling slats.

"Easy, Ellery," said Willow, made breathless by his brother's crushing strength.

And then Ellery swiped a big hand to Ashley, drawing all three brothers together in a mangled, uncomfortable knot tied by his grief. "I love y'all. So much," he said. Tears streamed down his reddened cheeks.

So close to seventeen in age and so much younger in heart than his sixteen years, Ellery squeezed his brothers and said, "I don't want it to be like this. I don't want him to be gone."

Ashley kissed Ellery atop his head. "I know," he said, only able to repeat what his mother had said.

"It's late," said Leigh. "Carolina and I will prepare the body."

Slowly, Ellery released his brothers, allowing them to disentangle. And while Willow drew away, Ashley found himself remaining close. For there was a sensation in holding Ellery that he had not known for years, a closeness he had forgotten. And now that he felt it again, he realized that he did not want to let it go. Ellery's crying, the innocent purity of it, fissured the cold resolve inside Ashley, and his own tears finally came in earnest.

Ellery's tight embrace returned, strong, unashamed in its aching. Ashley followed his brother's example and squeezed tightly, letting the manly dam surrounding his grief collapse, a spillway of tears rushed down his face.

"Don't go back," said Ellery. "Don't go back to St. Louis."

And it was a sudden realization that his brother was not only weeping for the loss of their father, but also afraid of what he knew would come to pass. Ashley had come. After the burial, he would go.

"Please stay with us."

Ashley said nothing, only held him. A part of him wanted to make that promise, but a greater portion kept him wise. He knew it was a promise he would not keep. He had known himself too long, and while leaving would hurt Ellery's feelings, making a false promise would shatter his heart. And though he was selfish as only young men can be, that he would not do. Not again.

"It's okay," he said. "Let's get some rest, El. You're tired. I'm tired."

Ellery drew back. "*Please,*" the word desperate, insistent. "No one else gets to leave home."

"My heart," said Leigh, sliding an arm between the two brothers. "Do not ask your brother to make promises when we are all so grieved. Your daddy is gone. Ashley is here. Let's get you to bed, and tomorrow we'll start the long, hard, and beautiful journey of saying our goodbyes."

She drew Ellery away, down the short hall to his bedroom.

Ashley dragged his sleeve across his wetted cheek and, when he looked up, saw red-faced Willow looking at him. There was a mixture of cold examination and fury in his brother's eyes. Ashley looked back, confused by his brother's mean gaze.

"You see," said Willow, breaking off for a moment. His jaw bulged. Relaxed. Bulged again. "You see now what your leaving did to him."

"I am not sorry that I left," said Ashley, beginning to repeat what he had said to his dying father. "But I am—"

"Of course," Will cut him off. "You've never been sorry for a goddamn thing in your whole goddamn life."

Ashley braced himself, his sadness swirling quickly to anger. "Careful."

"That's the word for it." Will's words came quickly. "That's how every single person in this family has treated you since as long as I can remember. Always careful not to make Ashley too mad. For who knows how he will respond. How reckless he might become."

"Will. You're tired."

"I surely am. Exhausted by the journey to come get you. Come get you. You, Ashley. I had to come get you when you should have been *here*."

Ashley set his face still as a stone wall. "Why? So I could raise horses and pigs? Marry a woman and listen to our kids scream all through the night?"

Willow's bony shoulders bobbed and he shook his head. His lips trembled. "No, goddamn you. Because you don't belong in St. Louis!"

From out of the kitchen came Carolina Ellison, stomping between them like a bull ready to whet its horns. "Now what in the hell is going on in here?"

Ashley glared at Willow.

Willow glared right back.

"There must be a misunderstanding," said Carolina, not quite flustered, but clearly perturbed. "Either you do not remember me well enough or the two of you are deaf, but when I ask a *fucking* question, I get a *fucking* answer."

Both brothers snapped their attention to meet the short woman's eyes.

"Oh good, you heard that did you? Now, your mother just lost the most important man in the world to her, not fifteen minutes ago. And here the two of you are arguing like a couple of jackasses while your little brother is sobbing at the loss of the last vestiges of his childhood." She swiveled, pointing a turgid finger at Willow. "You." It was a harsh whisper. Then she turned that jabbing digit toward Ashley. "You—both of you. Be fucking nice."

Willow slanted his eyes back over to Ashley. "Here," he said, "not St. Louis, not anywhere else. Here." It was his final word on the matter. He turned and pounded down the hall, entered his room and shut the door.

"What on earth did you say to him," said Carolina. "Get him so riled up about?"

"Doesn't matter."

"Brothers," she said. "They are the hardest to love."

Ashley was still boiling. The woman's voice barely registered to him. Who was Willow to tell Ashley where he belonged? If his little brother wanted to live and work and die all within a mile where he was born, well, that was his business. It would not be Ashley's. And at that moment he wanted to be out of the house, away from the farm, and in St. Louis even more than before he'd ever left.

"Ashley." Her voice was louder at first, clear. She said his name again, softer the second time. Then soft once more.

And when he saw that little smile in her round face, it made him relax.

"Brothers are the hardest to love, and they love the hardest. Hard enough to tell us what they feel, even if it's the thing they know we don't want to hear. My own brother taught me that."

He wasn't in a mood for another lecture. Certainly not after today, and certainly not from a woman he didn't know from Eve. Like the cards he'd been shuffling and reshuffling all evening, Ashley reshuffled the conversation. "Daddy told me you're here to collect on a debt. That you need help with something. He put that responsibility to me."

"Impatient and direct," she said, appraising him. "I do not begrudge those qualities in a person. Have some coffee with me. We'll talk."

Ashley followed her into the kitchen and sat down at the post oak pedestal table. She took the percolator and washed it out in a basin. "I mentioned my brother to you. His name is Hezekiah. He and I have been called to help mediate a problem between two families west of here in Kansas." She filled percolator with water and coffee grounds, then set it on the flat top of the potbelly stove warming the kitchen.

"What kind of problem?"

Carolina leaned against the wash cabinet. "A strange kind."

"Strange how?"

She opened her mouth into a big grin, as if ready to say something either funny or absurd. "Ashley, there is a world within our own that is very different from the one we perceive. I almost feel bad for what I'm about to tell you. . . and sort of glad, too. It's a funny thing, changing a person's life."

He furrowed his brow. "Ma'am, the man who brought me into the world left the world he brought me into not half an hour ago. So, I figure there's not much you can say that's going to change my life in a bigger way than that."

Carolina considered for a moment. "Perhaps."

Ashley guessed that was a pretty goddamn presumptuous answer.

It turned out that this guess was wrong as wrong could be.

The coffee came to brew. Carolina poured them both a cup and brought the steaming, tin vessels over to the table. Then, she settled her weight into a chair, curled a ribbon of her hair out of her tired eyes, and let out a deep breath. "The peregrine falcon is considered by many ornithologists to be the most adaptable bird of prey in the animal kingdom. Are you familiar with it?"

Ashley took a sip of coffee, which was too hot. "Round here we call them duck hawks. But yeah, sure."

"Duck hawk. . ." Carolina shook her head, finding something amusing. "If you meet my brother, you should say that directly to him. He will be interested to know it." She sipped her coffee. "It's a vicious predator. Big as a crow. Smart as the owl. And in a full dive, faster than hawk or eagle. Have you ever seen a peregrine dive?"

Come to think of it, he'd seen the bird many times in his life, but never during its plunge. He shook his head and drank the cooling coffee.

"I assure you, it is quite the sight. My brother and I have a deep admiration for its speed, its cunning, and the devastating effect it has when it strikes its intended target. Of all the hunters the world over, including humankind, the peregrine makes the most out of the gift it has been given. It is for that bird that my brother and I have named a growing outfit we run. A company of specialists, you might call them, who fly high, swoop fast, and annihilate threats before they even know what's coming."

"Annihilating threats, meaning people?"

"Some of the time."

"You run. . . an outfit of killers?" Looking at the woman he sniffed a laugh, the thought was ludicrous. "Hard to believe."

Though her grin remained, she became very serious. "And you, in your fancy French suit and your silk puff tie and your nickel-plated pistol, are the son of a hog farmer. Do not be too quick to decide what a thing is either by its appearance or its demeanor, Ashley. Like the peregrine, I may not look like much when I'm perched comfortably, but when I decide to fly. . ." She let the thought settle between them. "There are killers among our group, yes. And scientists. And riders of such navigation skill and endurance that they can travel distances neither you nor I would ever be able to accomplish. Other professions, too, ones that are beyond the understanding of such a man as you are. But I am going to change that." She took a long swallow of her coffee. "There are two families living along the Missouri, not too far from here, the Brohms and the McKennys. The four Brohm brothers are Dutch landowners of great wealth who have sectioned their stake into what they call the Little Kansas Barony. The Spanish government technically owns the land, but for reasons unknown to us, after their provincial Don died a few years back, the Brohms took over, and the Spanish did nothing to replace the official. They established a few towns and plantations."

"So, they're slave-owners," said Ashley.

"Surprisingly, no. The barony does not allow slavery, and it is known among American flesh traders that some who attempted to travel through the area, selling human lives, were executed, and the people in chains set free. In this way, the Brohms are more civilized than the politicians in our own country. They have their own codes and laws, all constructed and enforced by the four brothers and by the little militias set within each town. They are a strange little country, it seems."

Ashley shook his head, finding it difficult to take this all as seriously as the woman conveyed. "Is that it whole of it?"

"One more thing. . . the Brohms are lycan-thropes."

Ashley furrowed his brow, having never heard the word. "Is that their religion?"

Carolina looked up at the ceiling, considering and smiling at the notion. "In a way, yes. A lycanthrope is a human being who can change their shape. Increasing their strength, speed, and every measure of their aspect."

"I'm starting to see why maybe momma and daddy didn't want you coming around much or mention you over time. I've heard some wild ones in my time, Carolina, but hoowee," said

Ashley, drawing out the sound. "That's some ripe bullshi—"

"Do not patronize me," said Carolina. "If your parents did not educate you on such things, it wasn't because they thought they were crazy. It is because they wanted to protect their sons." Carolina's confidence didn't waver. And the look in her eyes, the surety of her words, none of them triggered the gambler's sense she was being false.

"Okay, I'll bite," he said. "Change their shape into what?"

"Like nothing you've ever seen. It varies for each lycanthrope, but they are all wolf-like, and there is a terrible strength in the strangeness of their proportion."

Ashley opened his mouth, but no words came out.

"Right," said Carolina. "Exactly."

"Change their shape. Their bodies."

"It's quite a stunning thing. Arresting."

"You've seen this?"

"Once," said Carolina.

"Still sounds like bullshit."

"I assure you, Ashley, it is anything but that. It is strange, but it's real. Having seen a lycanthrope in unbridled action, I can tell you—based on my own harrowing experience—there is no greater force of violence in observable nature."

"I. . . Y-you. Are you fucking with me right now?"

Carolina let out a long, almost exasperated sigh. "No. Your reaction is that of every other man, believing nothing until he can see it for himself, until he has *evidence* of a thing. Men struggle to trust, because they cannot trust themselves, and because they have a great speculation living within them. But it is real, Ashley, take my word for it. If we do our jobs well, we will both be lucky to avoid seeing that transformation for ourselves. Now, the McKenny's—"

"Wait." Ashley raised his palm. "You're trying to tell me that there are people in the world who can change their—"

"Change their shape," said Carolina, earnestly and without any desperation for him to believe her, as if she were stating an irrefutable fact. And this was what began to convince Ashley. "Now, may I, with the McKenny's and the problem?"

"Sure, but you can damn well bet I'm gonna have a cigarette, weird as this conversation is getting." He reached into his pocket. "Jesus Christ," he mumbled as he rolled a fresh cigarette, "fucking abolitionist wolf-men in the goddamn Spanish frontier."

"The McKennys recently immigrated to America from Ireland," said Carolina. "They are more a clan than a family. Well. . . with the condition they share with the Brohms, you could call them—"

"A pack," Ashley said and snapped a match to life, bringing it close to the cigarette. "It's a fucking wolf pack." He sucked the cylinder to life, breathing in the smoke.

"You catch on quick."

"One pack comes into the territory of the other. So it's a range dispute."

"And that means a war. My brother and I have been asked to negotiate a peace between the two parties," she said. "As outside, independent parties."

"Or they're gonna go to war with each other."

"What a glory it is to be comprehended."

Ashley blew out the smoke. "Why did you come here? What were you going to ask my father for and why this moment?"

Carolina furrowed her brow at him. "I'm surprised you would ask—"

"He doesn't know." It was the voice of his mother.

Ashley turned and looked to the cut of the doorway, where the slight, tired woman leaned against the frame. "None of the boys know," she said.

There was a tone inside his mother's voice he'd never heard. The sound of a secret kept and the shame of keeping it. Inside Ashley Sutliff, a stone rolled over the high precipice of his heart and collided with his stomach. "Don't know what?" he asked, sharper than he intended.

"Leigh," said Carolina, making the woman's name long. Disappointed.

"Don't know what?" Ashley said again.

His mother looked to Carolina, sadness in her eyes.

"I love you dearly," said Carolina. "And I loved your husband. If I had known you were going to keep this from—"

"Ashley," Leigh said. "I want to talk to Carolina now."

"Hold on, mother. I—"

"Son."

"No, I'm not going to be—"

"Ashley Forrest Sutliff, this is my house," his mother said. "And while I have never asked for all in it be my way, in this way I will."

That sent a trill of frustration into his ears, a fresh anger. But before he could talk back, Carolina spoke.

"Your mother and I have a lot to talk about, Ashley. And we need to prepare the body for burial. It's late. You're tired. Do as your mother says."

Inside the little bedroom where he had spent the whole sum of his life, Willow stared out the window, watching the snow fall through the darkness. The fiery glow from the windows of the house strained against the night. A fresh powder, drifting gently, covering everything in the downy blanket of winter. He thought about the grave, glad that he and Ellery had covered it with buffalo hide, pulled taut and staked to the ground, to keep all moisture out of the fresh grave waiting for their father's coffin. Along with the man inside.

The man inside.

He recalled his father's strong hands, thickly veined, always active. The sound of his voice, baritone, never quite a bass. And the tenor of his mercurial moods, which swayed between extremes, never finding a middle ground within himself. He was a man of great rapture and terrible sorrow, happiest when holding his wife, never more despondent than the day Ashley had left.

Will's sight shifted, blurring the snow outside, so that his focus came to rest on the candle-lit image of his face in the dark mirror-black of the glass. He saw his father's despondency there in his own features. And he saw himself, red-eyed and haggard, looking so far beyond his seventeen years. Shocked, he looked away. For the image of himself brought into his mind the face of the man who had educated him on hard work, on how to shave, and on when to fight and what was worth fighting for. Where would he go now to find all the answers to manly questions and seek out the wisdom that only a father can pass to a son? Would he live the rest of his life as an incomplete portrait of who he wanted to become?

Where do sons flee when their father's take all their wisdom with them? And where do fathers go. . . where did anyone go when they died? To heaven? Into a coffin? Into the darkness of the hereafter or just the darkness living within the ground?

His father had been gone for less than an hour, and all he could think of was the forever waiting ahead where the man would not be. The world—his world—would now exist with this empty space so much larger than the size of the person who had filled it in waking life. And in this way, though he would not understand it until just before his final day on earth, Willow felt the sorrow his father had known two years ago—the day Ashley had ridden for St. Louis. The shattering heartbreak that comes with saying goodbye, and all the love that leaves with the person you love most.

Ashley had always been his mother's favorite, but it was Willow who knew his father's ardor best. The second son had made the man most proud. Though he'd never said it, his child saw it in his brown eyes and his unique smile, heard it in every, "Good job, son."

From outside the room there came a series of raised voices. Then, the pounding of heavy footfalls down the hall. The opening and shutting of the room across the hall. Ashley's room.

Good, thought Will.

"I hope she chews you out real good," he said to himself.

He got up to rejoin his mother and hear what Ashley had done now. Support her. Whatever their mother had chided his brother about, he probably deserved it. Willow had taken only a few steps down the hall when he heard his mother's voice from the kitchen: ". . .I don't want them to know."

He froze. Listened.

"It was a long time ago," Carolina said, consoling. "They would understand."

"You always say people will understand."

"I say what I believe."

"Well, you're wrong. And I don't want my children knowing that I associated with those people or that society or. . . or any of it."

"Your children love you," said Carolina. "How can you think they wouldn't—"

"I will not be lectured at."

There was a pause. The sound of a cup sliding along the kitchen table.

Willow took two careful steps toward the voices.

"Ashley will want to know, Leigh. And I don't think it's fair not to tell him why he's going up the river with me."

His mother scoffed. "There is nothing fair about raising a child, and—"

"He's a man. Not a child."

"He's my child," she said, her voice sharp. "If you plan to speak a word of it, Carolina, you might as well get your shit and ride off now and never think of coming back."

"Leigh. . ."

"I mean it."

"But you were just a girl. Your father raised you in the Prometheus Society. Hezekiah and I were willing participants, and we need to make recompense after escaping their lies. You have got to let go of this. . . this shame for the things you had no choice in," said Carolina. "You met Forrest. Escaped with us. Found love. Look at where love's long journey has brought you, far and away from that cult. And. . . and I love you, Leigh. My brother also. We love you and your boys love you. Though it may be difficult at the moment, in the face of loss, but love surrounds you, no matter what happened before. No matter what's ahead."

Willow found himself stirred, wanting to go to his mother and wrap his arms around her and hold her close. To say nothing and let all of his care and protection and admiration for her flow out of his heart and into her own. But he just stood there, hiding in the midnight shadows soaking the hallway, listening as his mother began to cry. Her sobbing was soft, quiet in a way that revealed both her great strength and even greater self-control.

"I know," said Carolina. "And I am so sorry."

Her voice was barely audible when she said, "I don't want him to be gone. I just kept staring at that door for weeks and weeks, waiting to see him walk out healthy and strong, giving his smile in the way he only gave it to me. But. . ."—her voice deepened, became raw—"he's gone and I. . . I. . . All he ever wanted was me, Carolina."

"I know."

"We saved each other from the world. Chose each other over all the rest."

"Yes. And I believe it's only a small but hard goodbye. This life is only a passing thing before what comes after."

"Only for a piece," said his mother. "Only for a time."

"Are you sure. . ." Carolina's words faltered for a moment. "Are you absolutely sure about Ashley? It's dangerous, and I cannot promise his safety." Another pause. "Or his survival."

Safety, thought Willow. *Survival?* What in the

hell had Ashley gotten himself into with Carolina Ellison in the short time since their argument. And, more than that, what was his mother hiding?

"He's a grown man," his mother said, sadness in her voice. "It's entirely up to him. Seeing him today. . .". There was a little sniff of laughter, though there was little joy in it. "Seeing that boy come home today made me about as happy as happiness gets. I knew how much it meant to Forrest for him to be able to say good-bye, and to pass on this debt."

Debt? What debt?

"Ashley has too much of me in him," she continued. "And right now, he's become the kind of man that makes me most afraid."

"A gambler?"

"The gambling I understand. The want for St. Louis and big dreams, too. No, he's become a man without a purpose. Aimless. Rolling along life's river without a way to go other than that which circumstance provisions. Ellery wants to make everyone happy. Willow clings to duty and labor and wants to grow this place into something bigger and grander than me and Forrest ever did. But Ashley. . ." She let out a big sigh. "A man without a vision for who he can become ends up poor and alone and begging for someone to respect them. Men like that end up mean and vindictive, and Ashley is already mean enough. I believe that you and Hezekiah could use a man like him and, moreover, that Ashley needs a greater vision of the world—to find a way to make a mark on it."

"You think he'll agree to it?" asked Carolina.

"I do not know. When it comes to that child, I have given up on guessing."

"But not given up on him."

"No," she said. "Never."

There was a quiet space where all Willow could think about was how simple she had made his dreams sound. She had been correct about them, flattering even, but somehow it made him feel. . .well, as small as the quiet moment that stretched out. If there was a family debt to be paid, well, he'd be damned if he'd let Ashley be the one to see it paid. His mother put too much stock in her eldest. Whatever road was required to see the family name upheld, Will would be the one to see it through.

He slipped back down the hall into his room and shut the door softly, turning the knob so that the latch did not click. He sat once again at his desk in front of the window and, watching the snow flurry, considered the work he'd need to ask Ellery to do: the bare minimum required to ensure the horses were taken care of, and the pigs slopped, and the barn roof repaired before moisture rotted the whole thing through, and all the little things one young man could accomplish alone. The list grew long, likely too long. His mind grew hazy, and the snow drifts seemed to blend into one white canvas. Mentally and emotionally exhausted, he went to his bed and lay down.

Sleep did not come quickly and when it did, it was dreamless and too shallow to provide rest.

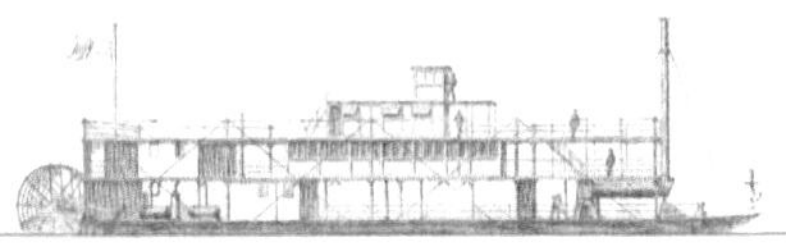

Sutliff Acreage
Ste. Genevieve County,
Missouri

Ashley awoke in the middle of the night, not knowing how long he had slept, his eyes heavy. Every joint was stiff from the cold that had found a way under his bed sheets and through the thin fabric of his old nightshirt. He'd found the nightshirt in the bedroom drawer, untouched since the day he left. The little fireplace opposite his bed was mostly black, spotted with red embers. Shivering, he kneeled to stoke the fire. He found a patch of heat beneath the coal, added wood and breath and careful attention until the fire crawled out from its hiding place and, showing its fullness, lit the room. Warmth creeped into his hands, which he rubbed before the fire until his knuckles no longer ached and his shivering subsided. Late unto morning, Ashley cleaned his boots and brushed his trousers. Then he warmed water in his little basin to wash his face and hair, and shaved using instruments he'd left in the wash cabinet years ago. Hair slicked back, smooth-faced with a clean shave, he looked at himself in the little shaving mirror. His eyes were bright and awake, severe and shining with firelight.

Outside the east-facing window, the sun was rising. It threw its unique golden cream color through the ring of trees surrounding the Sutliff acreage, lengthening their shadows so that their spindly branches near touched the house. The black of the shadows set upon the golden snow, dyed by sunlight, was a sight that gripped Ashley by the heart. And for a moment, all the beauty of that land made him forget about cards and money and all the dreams that lived in St. Louis. He had learned to rope and ride in that field, had dashed among those familiar shadows in the summer mornings of his youth. And it was beyond that forest ring, far beyond the shadows, that he had run and run and run from home into a thunderstorm, and had gotten lost.

It was his father who found him the next day.

They didn't speak for a week after.

They would never speak again.

He shoved away the memory and what today would mean and leaned his consideration on what Carolina had said at the kitchen table. Lycanthropes — what a fucking silly notion. And then for his mother to interrupt the way that she did, to be so intent on keeping secret whatever it was she was hiding. Had they robbed a bank? Crossed the wrong people? Perhaps his mother had shot and killed a person of great importance. The rogue inside him liked that idea best.

He wanted to know very badly, but he convinced himself not to ask. Not today.

Ashley slipped on his shirt and trousers, coat and polished black boots. And he walked out of his room to the sound of coffee percolating from the kitchen and the nail-driving hammer swings of Ellery finishing a coffin outside.

Ashley went into the kitchen, as he had done a thousand and more times before this morning, to find his mother standing over the stove cooking eggs in the big iron skillet. And like so many times before, and yet not in over two years, he kissed her on the cheek and said, "Morning, mother." She leaned into the kiss, never turning her head from the eggs, as if they had not missed a single day since the last completion of this sacred moment.

"Good morning, son," she said, completing the ritual. "Coffee is ready. Breakfast in a bit." She wiped her hands on the white apron embroidered with drooping bluebell flowers. "Your brother could use some help outside."

Ashley filled a tin cup with coffee and, dragging a gentle hand across his mother's shoulders as he walked out of the kitchen, said, "Yes ma'am."

Near the porch, Martin stood rigged to the hay wagon, his halter rope tied off at the front porch hitch. Ashley walked out into the chilly, bright winter morning and, crunching through the ankle-deep snow, made his way to the barn.

The doors were open, the barn alley all shot through with light. Ellery, with a single stroke, drove a nail to secure the final wall of the simple, pine box set atop the worktable. His brother wore only trousers over red long johns. The sleeves were rolled up, revealing near hairless forearms each thick as cylinder of firewood and fingernails bright and clean, as their mother expected.

Ashley said nothing at first, looking over his brother's work. He ran his fingertips over the wood. The planks comprising the vessel's shape had been cut to perfection and sanded smooth as snakeskin.

"You're too late, if you've come to help." Ellery tapped a nail once to make it stand erect, then once more, so that it never moved again. He wiped his arm across his brow, though there was no sweat Ashley could see. "Nice of you to bring me some coffee though."

Ashley smiled and relinquished the cup. "Mother's making breakfast."

"Like every morning." Ellery sipped the coffee. And then his eyes drifted from Ashley, a thought taking him to another place.

"No," said Ashley, knowing his brother's feeling. "Not like every other morning."

Ellery set the blue tin cup on top of the yellow-gold pine coffin and rested his knuckles on his hips. "It's ready for Daddy."

"It's perfect, brother."

Ellery set his face somewhere between the sternness of consideration and the dissatisfaction of a frown. "You leaving today? After?"

"That depends. Carolina asked me to help her on an errand, and Daddy insisted that I do it."

"Well, I'm sure that displeased you. You come home to say goodbye, and our father gives you a chore he knows you'll hate."

Ashley thought a moment. "I do not know that I hate it, Ellery."

"Hmm." Ellery picked up his coffee cup from the coffin. "You never enjoyed his appointed chores before."

"I didn't say I enjoyed it. I'd rather he was still here to argue with about it."

His brother nodded. "I know."

Ashley ran a hand over the coffin again. "It really is perfect. He would be proud."

"I hope so," said Ellery, the little frown sliding into the familiar Sutliff family grin. "He's the one who taught me how to make things. It feels like a gift, a last gift, to show him that I was listening, watching, paying attention, even when he thought I wasn't."

Their mother's voice came bellowing from the front porch: "Boys!"

"Remember when she asked Daddy for a dinner bell?" asked Ellery.

"Sure," said Ashley, turning to see his mother heading back into the house. "One of the few things he refused her."

"He told me why. Said one of his favorite things was to hear her voice pealing across the yard, calling him in."

As they walked back across the yard, his little brother threw a massive hand onto his shoulder. Hugged him in their gait. "My god, is it good to see you." He pulled Ashley tighter, cinching him comedically close. "Maybe this time I don't let you leave."

"Bigger men have tried, little brother. And all of them meaner than you."

Ellery laughed, and they walked together, close as brothers have ever been.

The kitchen was warm and buzzing with activity, a strong contrast to the solemnity of the previous night. His mother was setting a plate of sizzling bacon and sunny-side-up eggs next to a pile of buttermilk biscuits busting at the seams, their tops golden as a butter stick. Carolina was peering through a pair of readers perched on her nose, turning the page on a leather-bound volume titled *Unaussprechlichen Kulten*, whatever the hell that meant. Willow was shifting and stretching around his mother, placing plates at each of the chairs around the table. There was the rattle of crockery dishes set on wood, the tinny echo of silverware placed beside them, all beneath the low, persistent humming of the potbelly stove's fire.

"Everyone have a seat," their mother said.

"There aren't enough chairs," said Willow. "I'll stand and eat."

"Nonsense," she replied. "Sit down, honey. I'm not hungry, and besides, I want to talk to you boys."

The brothers Sutliff, all three, sat at the table together. Ellery began to dish out heaps of eggs. Willow drank his coffee while reaching over for a single biscuit. Ashley reached into his coat pocket, produced his tobacco, and began to roll a cigarette.

Carolina sipped at her coffee, keeping quiet, reading.

Their mother placed her hands against the wash counter, looking fresher than the night before. Her eyes were bright, hair pulled back in a bun, and she was smiling a tired smile. "It makes my heart so glad to see the three of you around this table." She shifted her eyes to Ashley. "Do not light that cigarette while other people are eating, son."

Ashley lifted his eyebrow, shrugged, and put the cigarette down.

"Thank you. Now, today is going to be a hard day for everyone, and I just wanted to say. . ."

Ashley noticed how hard she was squeezing the counter, the whites of her knuckles visible.

"I mean—"

Ellery said, "It's okay, Momma."

"No, I know. I just wanted you to know how proud I am of each of you. How much it means to see you all here, and how much your daddy would have loved to see you all together too. And before the burial today, I wanted to tell you that Ms. Ellison here requires our help. She came hoping your father could help, but now. . . now that he is gone. . ." She pressed through the grief inching into her voice. "Now that your father is gone, the requirement falls to you. She needs capable and trustworthy people where she is going, and because I am afraid to send one of you alone—even you, Ashley, with your worldly experience—I have decided to send all of you."

Ellery stopped eating, mouth hanging open like a cow with a cud.

Willow slashed his gaze to Ashley.

Ashley looked to Willow, then to his mother. "What about the farm?"

Willow sniffed a laugh. "That's rich coming from you."

"Will," his mother warned.

"Despite the source of the opinion, I agree," said Will. "There's too much work and upkeep that needs to be done—"

"I'm sorry," she cut in. "Are you about to tell me all that needs to be done to keep this place upright?"

"No, I only mean that—"

"Yes, please, son. Tell me how the hogs and horses need to be fed. How the barn needs a patch. You should remember that before you were of working age, it was your father and *me* who worked on the barn, back when it was only a foundation. I cut the wood for the chair you are sitting in, all while making your meals and tending your needs with Ellery here still on the tit. I will do the work, as I have before. If I need help, I'll hire out one of the Johnson boys."

Will's jaw clenched, relaxed, clenched again.

"I am not asking you to go, Will. I'm telling you."

"Mother," said Ashley, "Will's just concerned. Like we all are."

"Don't speak for me," said Will.

Now it was Ashley whose ire flared. "Brother,

I've had it up to here with that tone and that attitude."

"Both of y'all knock it off," Ellery said, glaring at Ashley then Willow.

"*Boys,*" their mother's voice was sharp. Final.

There was a passing moment, and then the woman who had given all three men in the room life shattered before their very eyes. It was abrupt, crushing. Leigh Sutliff began to sob.

Ellery rose first, followed by Willow. Ashley was so shocked that he failed to move at all.

"No," she said Leigh, lifting a palm. "Sit, goddamn it, and eat the breakfast I made for you!"

Ellery turned back to his chair, throwing mean glances to his brothers. Willow sat too, eyes facing the table.

"If you say go, mother," said Ashley. "We go." He heard the words before he knew he was saying them. Decided before he knew he was making a decision.

She wiped her eyes with the back of her hand, brushing away tears she refused to let fall. "Damn all this. Damn sickness and time. I will never forgive God for it."

Carolina closed her book and set it on the table. She rose and went to their mother, and pulled her into an embrace. "You need to rest," she said.

"I know. But not before Forrest."

Though Carolina was facing away from the brothers, she said, "Boys, please, bring in the coffin and place your father inside." She gently stroked Leigh's hair, then with delicate fingers brushed the tears from her cheeks.

Each of the remaining men of the Sutliff family name saw the open grief that had wholly possessed their mother, and as a collective stood up and went about the awful work no son should ever know but too often does – to carry the body of the man who raised them to a final resting place.

They brought the coffin to the porch, each carrying a corner, and then went to their father's bedroom.

Captain Forrest M. Sutliff lay in the bed, unmoving.

Ashley took a deep breath and looked at the empty vessel of his father, which they would soon place into an empty coffin, in an empty space in the ground. filling the earth with their father and the portions of themselves he had taken with him. The parts that only he could give life.

With six arms lifting as one, the brothers Sutliff moved in unison, setting the body upon a slender board. Then they carried the body suited nicely in a white shirt and black frock coat the man had rarely worn. In slow, reverent procession, they moved out of the bedroom and through the kitchen, where Ashley's mother stood near the potbelly stove, one clenched fist holding a little silk handkerchief too small to hide her mouth and quivering chin. They moved around the post oak pedestal table and down the l hall, through the living room and out the front door. There, the sons of Captain Sutliff, again moving as a collective, laid the body to rest inside the coffin.

Ashley took his father's wrists into his hands and crossed them over his breast. Ellery stepped off the porch into the snow, where he gathered the coffin lid.

"Wait," said Willow, and went into the house. When he came back out, he was holding their father's black felt hat. He set it atop the man's crossed arms, crooked at first, but he turned it slightly so that the brim set straight.

"Good," said Ashley. "That's just right."

Ellery set the coffin lid to lean against the house, and then he looked down with admiration upon the face of his father. The face none of them would ever see again.

Their mother and Carolina stepped onto the porch. Ashley saw that they were holding hands, his mother's knuckles as white as they had been on the kitchen counter.

The stillness of the cold winter day lay over all time.

"We love you, Daddy," said Ellery.

"Yes we do," said Leigh. She then nodded at Ellery.

The youngest son slid the coffin lid into place, and handed a hammer and nails to Ashley. "You first. Leave a few for the rest of us though."

Each brother went, one by one and in one accord, sealing the coffin for as long as the well-sanded wood would keep.

The brothers lifted the coffin into the flatbed hay wagon, sliding it forward. Ashley took Martin's halter rope from the hitch, patted the gelding's nose, and said, "Nice and easy, boy."

Like those following behind, Martin seemed in no rush to pull his cargo to the plot. But he did his work all the same in the crisp morning, the sun rising bright as a candle flame in a sky bluer and clearer than Ashley had ever known. The color of it would run through his memory for the rest of his life.

The Sutliff brothers, all three, rolled the buffalo tarp up like a scroll, opening the grave to the light of the sun and the once-in-a-lifetime blue. Ropes were laid across the gulf, the coffin laid atop them, and slowly, hand over hand, the coffin was set within the grave. The ropes were discarded where they rested, never again to be tied.

Ashley stood there beside his mother. Tears spilled from her cheeks to join with the snow at their feet. He put an arm around her shoulder, pulling her close.

"It's okay," she said. More to him than to herself, it seemed.

"If all your grief is too great," said Carolina, politely, "I am happy to say a word."

"Thank you, ma'am," said Willow, interjecting. "I will."

Willow had thought about it all through the night, what he would say at this moment. The moment when his family needed him to be strongest. At his best.

"You were the most important man in our lives," he began, feeling the words shake. "You always will be. You showed us how to love a woman in the way you loved mother. You raised three imperfect boys into imperfect men, who are closer to perfect because of you. There are no words for the fullness of our gratitude. No greater way to express our love for you other than to give that love back into the world that was never worthy of you."

And Willow took a breath, pausing as Ashley's arm curled over his shoulder. It was at this touch that dutiful son began to find a way to forgive the prodigal first-born.

"We love you," said Ellery, stepping closer to Willow.

"Away have," said Ashley. "Always will."

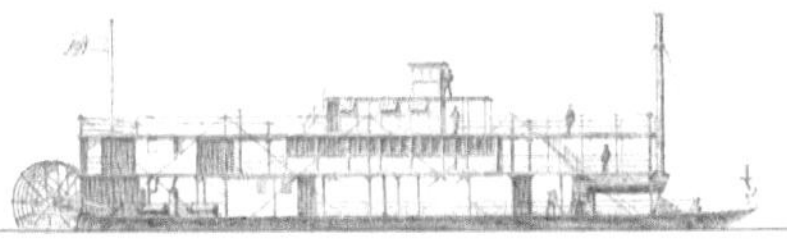

SUTLIFF ACREAGE
JANUARY 11, 1845

They buried their father and mourned his passing for the rest of that morning. By the time the sun was on the downturn of the day, making a slope of the sky, Ellery and Willow, and even Ashley, were out in the eastern pasture, watching the meager number of the Sutliff family remuda chop up the hoarfrost with their running. The afternoon was chill, and the wind blew the scent of aspens over the whited landscape, where Martin and Fairbanks, a blonde-maned fiery paint mustang of chestnut and white, chased after each other, playing in the snow. They were chuffing and whining at each other, which to Ashley always seemed like two friends cussing each other in jest. And he watched them, along with the mares Ellery and Willow inspected for possible sale. Both of them were good riders, but horsetraders not so much. And in watching them it gave him a reason not to look back at the little mound of dirt newly risen to the north.

Ashley smoked a rolled cigarette as his brothers looked into the teeth, mostly pretending to know what to look for in the mouth of a mare who was having none of it. He was laughing when he heard Carolina come crunching up behind him.

"How's mother," he said, still watching his brothers pretend to be horsemen of educated quality.

"Finally resting. She was up all the night, grieving and doing what was required of her."

"Did you convince her to send all three of us with you?" asked Ashley.

"No." Carolina pointed to his brothers, who were now struggling to keep the mare from pulling away entirely. "That's not gonna work."

"Yeah," he said. "But they don't know that."

In the distance, Willow shouted, "Now, goddamn it, Ellery. I said hold 'er still!"

"I'm tryin'!" Ellery boomed.

"Whatever it's worth," Carolina said, "if it's worth anything at all, I told her not to send all three of you, that I needed only one man as capable as your daddy was. She said none of the three of you were that, but all together you might come close."

Ashley took the final pull from his cigarette. "Well, if anyone would know. . ."

Carolina turned to face him. "We're gonna leave tomorrow. I'm already a day behind schedule, and my brother hates to wait. Now, we'll stop off in St. Louis, but not so long that you'll think about abandoning ship and going back to your revelries."

"I promised Daddy I would help you."

"Promised." She sniffed a laugh. "I could fill a thousand books with all the broken promises of men."

"You'll find my brothers and me different."

Carolina shook her head, still smiling that little, mean smile of hers. "All men think they're different, and that's exactly how they're all the same."

"And here you are, asking for their help."

"I've never said men are useless. I just know the things they're good for."

The mare jerked away from Willow. "Ellery!"

"Shit," he hollered. "Aye, goddamn."

The blue-gray mare pulled free and, painted gold in the January sun, took off for the barn, likely for the hay.

Carolina laughed. Ashley, too.

"Good thing I don't need horsemen," she said.

"And what *do* you need us for," asked Ashley. "You have yet to specify."

Carolina patted him on the shoulder, a feast of mirth in her eyes. "For the one thing your mother has assured me you're all three mostly good at—violence."

In the late afternoon, they joined together for an early supper of steak, potatoes, and carrots, and pearl onions smothered in a bacon-grease gravy. They ate like ticks sucking on a purebred hound. In the middle of the meal, Ashley found himself thinking two things: one, he couldn't remember the last time he'd had a steak; two, how alive the table was with conversation. The difference in tension. His mother seemed rested and, while still sad, somehow smiling. She teased them all, reached over to squeeze their hands from time to time, and got teary-eyed all over again when she said just how proud their father would have been.

Carolina ate quickly so that she could begin to pack and make ready for the trip to St. Louis and connect with her brother. But that was hours away, Ashley thought, and the conversation around the dinner table was all that he wanted to focus on. And for a moment, just for this moment in time, he found it within himself to ask the question, *Why did I ever leave?*

"You're sure you don't want us to stay until tomorrow?" asked Willow, concerned. Always concerned. "I can go talk to the Johnsons, make sure they're willing—"

"I am sure, son," their mother said. She set her napkin on her plate, straightened in her chair. "Now, I want you boys, all three, to remember. . . I am letting Carolina borrow you. Not keep you. You will be exposed to different things on this journey. Strange things that will, without question, change your life." She turned to focus on her youngest. "Ellery, you listen to Willow and to Ashley. Don't be stubborn about it."

"Yes, ma'am."

She looked to Willow. "Don't boss Ellery around."

He rolled his eyes. "Mother—"

"I mean it, Willow. He's his own man. You can *advise* him, but the world isn't the farm, and he has a good head on his shoulders." And then she looked to Ashley. Her mouth tightened at one end, drawing the wrinkles smooth, her lips appearing as they had in his youth.

And just as when he had arrived back home, Ashley found he could not meet his mother's gaze. It was too fierce, the emotion she carried finding its way into him and reaching a place deep within—much too deep for his heart to withstand. She had always had this power over him and, in using it sparingly, it never shrank in its seismic effect.

"Take care of your brothers," she said. "It falls to you. No one else."

"Falls to him?" said Willow, an insult wearing the costume of a question.

She ignored his brother. Only waited for a moment and then said, "Ashley."

"I hear you, Mother."

"Son."

His heart swelled at the sweetness of her tone, at all the love residing within that delicate command. And he looked up, met her springtime gaze, and said, "I will."

Willow gathered clothes, his gun-cleaning kit, and skinning knife, and set it all within a bedroll, tucked in a way that would make it easy enough to reach, quick to get to. In his saddlebag, he placed a bar of soap, his razor, a whetstone, and a small portion of money, just in case. He looked out his bedroom window at the sunset fire lining the tops of the roundel of trees. Night was coming and he did not like riding in the dark, but Carolina had made it clear that they must make all haste to reach St. Louis as quickly as possible.

Outside, his family waited on the porch. Ashley had also packed his things in a tight bedroll, which he had tied down on the mean-as-hell blue-gray mare that had refused inspection earlier in the day. Ellery's big American gelding stood next to Martin, loaded down with a bedroll and saddlebags at both the front and the back. His brother's shotgun was set on one side, and his rifle sleeved on the other.

Carolina rode out of the barn, sitting side-saddle on a fine-looking Appaloosa the color of mud with a brilliant snow-cap running from rump to hock. Watching the big woman ride side-saddle was to witness grace in a rider he had never seen before.

Ashley and Ellery said their goodbyes to their mother, both kissing her before they went to their horses. She said something to each of them in a low voice, but Willow could not hear what. And when he went to say goodbye to her, she pulled his tall frame to bend, so that she might kiss him, too.

"I love you, mother," he said, as he had ten-thousand times before, never meaning it more than he did at that moment.

"I love you, too," she said and kissed him on the cheek. Before he could pull away, she gripped his shoulder, keeping him close. "Forgive your brother," she said. "Take care of Ellery. And remember what Daddy said before you went to St. Louis: 'Only be as mean as you have to be.'"

"Yes ma'am," he said, wrapping his lanky arms around her, trying to instill upon her a protection that would last as long as he was required to be gone.

When he stepped away, he dragged one hand along hers, so that their fingertips touched at the last of their embrace.

He mounted Martin and turned the gelding to face the scarlet sun of early evening, sweeping his eyes along the northern portion of acreage where his father's grave lay, just in eyeshot.

"Be safe," his mother said. "I'll be waiting. Eagerly."

"I'll have them back in no time, friend," said Carolina, riding up, then stopping next to Martin. "Come on, boys," she said, smiling a cat's broad, mischievous grin and looking younger than her years. "Gonna show you things you've never seen."

And she barreled forward with a happy yip loud and carefree.

Ellery took off with her, waving his hat high in the air and yelling goodbye.

Ashley shook his head and said, "We'll be back," as if they were running to town for nothing more than a sack of flour, and he rode on, leaving Willow last.

Martin, ever-eager to run, snorted and pawed the snow. He begged to have the length of his neck, to chew-up the distance between himself and wherever the destination might be, but Willow held the gelding fast, turned to look at his mother.

"Go on," she said. "If you let her win, you'll never hear the end of it."

He had said "I love you" and refused to say goodbye, and so he was not sure what to say in that moment; life compelled him forward, though he felt required to stay.

"It's okay," his mother said. "It's only for a piece."

Willow swallowed hard. "Only for a time."

She kissed her fingertips, then turned her hand so that all the love in that kiss turned itself upon him.

"Okay, boy," he said. And with a "Let's go," he squeezed Martin, unbinding the gelding from restraint.

By the time Willow and Martin reached the shallow creek, burning like a stream of heavenly gold along the unmarked barrier of the Sutliff acreage, they had overtaken both brothers. Carolina, however, was a different story. Splashing through the waters, never slowing in the spray, she came up the little embankment and then pressed hard for the snow-powdered trail, which was a straightaway cut near all the way to the landing.

Her Appaloosa might have been more adroit and better handled, but Martin, when given nothing but space, had been fashioned by God to champion over such uninterrupted lengths. Willow posted high, settled into Martin's gait.

Rider and gelding became one locomotive force, each trusting the other. "Yeah! Yeah, boy, here we go now!"

Carolina looked back, smiling, and upon seeing the gelding reeling closer she split the concert of their running with the sound of rapturous glee. From side-saddle, she slipped her boot from the stirrup, took hold of the pronounced saddle horn, and let her feet hit the ground so that the momentum from the horse sent her back up. Her skirts fluttered in the open air for a moment, revealing the chicken-feather whites of her bloomers, and she then came to straddle her saddle, leaning forward in the English fashion. And then it was her turn to pour on the speed.

There was a competitiveness living inside of Willow Sutliff, as it forever would be for all middle-born children, and he would be goddamned if he was going to be beat in a horse race by any living person, and so he whooped and hollered for Martin to show that Appaloosa who was boss. Like one storm chasing another, Martin thundered, chasing the lighting speed of Carolina. And it was a minute, perhaps more, when he saw Carolina throw her head back, her brown hair all wind-tossed like a flag raveled to tatters in the fading light of day.

She slowed her gait, and the Appaloosa's rump bounced as the gallop ebbed to trot. The woman was laughing wildly, a hearty sound that grew louder as he came to ride broadside to her. He saw Carolina's wide, happy eyes, the sheen of sweat, and the absolute grandeur of a smile never before seen. And that's when he knew, for the first time in his life, he had met someone who understood this moment as well as he did. A moment when, inside his own mind he was able to connect, thinking, *Oh, you're just like me.*

"That Martin," said Carolina. "I'd heard tell, but my word. . . I thought I'd leave you all in the mud." She laughed again. The sound hearty and unashamed. "Look at him, he's barely even lathered."

"He's the best," said Willow. "But I will say, that was quite the little saddle-hop change. Only ever seen that once at a circus show, years back."

"Oh, my daddy taught me that at thirteen," she said, pretending it was no big deal. "Anyone can do it if they practice long enough, and are willing to break an ankle. . . twice."

Willow laughed.

And when he did, something shifted in her face, as if the sound surprised her. "I'm so glad it amuses you. I will have you know that twenty years ago, it was not funny at all. I was on crutches for six weeks the first time, five for the second."

"Well, I don't figure I'll be trying it any time

soon." He turned to look back. "I don't see. . . Ah, there they are, just coming over that ridge."

"You're an uncommonly gifted horseman on a straightaway," said Carolina. "Can you cut and work on a horse as well as you gallop?"

Willow settled back in the saddle. "Martin does the work. I just keep steady and stay out of the way."

"Careful, you say that to the wrong woman, and they'll scoop you up with that attitude." She wiped her brow on the sleeve of her coat.

Will didn't know what to say at that, so he did as he usually did, saying nothing at all.

They rode alongside each other with the sun fading and the twilight purpling the sky, the fingers of winter searching for the gaps in his coat. Carolina Ellison talked like no woman he'd ever met before. Not that he had met many women worth talking to, or really that many women at all. There was a warmth to her, a bluster, a confidence. An undeniable pressure of personality that got him to open up and talk when he had always considered himself more a listener. She opened up too, telling him about her conversation with Ashley, about the Little Kansas Barony, and about the strange, shape-changing aristocrats making trouble for their Germanic, immigrant kin.

He found it easy to take her at her word. And part of him questioned the reality of what she was saying certainly, found it hard to believe. But his mother had believed this woman, his father, too. And for Willow Sutliff, their belief was plenty enough belief for him. "I hear you, and will be glad to help in any way I can," Willow said when the woman finally paused to gather his appraisal of all she had said.

"In all my life I have never seen someone take in the story of our work and purpose so easily, Willow Sutliff. Most people outright dismiss such things, rail against them. Deny." She smiled, like she felt sorry for those who had never known or would never know what she knew. "There are lots of things me, my brother, and our company know about that would turn you white as a summer cloud. But if we're lucky, you won't see anything much at all on this trip— at least, not if my dim-witted brother, who has a mind for ciphering and negotiation, I will admit, does his job well enough."

"And if he fails?"

"That cannot be allowed to happen," she said, filled with insistence. "My brother will not be happy that I am bringing three young Sutliffs when he asked me to bring one old one. But he will not be angry that each of you are capable with a gun, because if he does fail at negotiating a peace, well, then you should know: the trick to killing a werewolf is to kill it before or during its transformation. The moment the transformation is over, your best hope is to run in the opposite direction of everyone else and pray to God it goes for them and not you."

"Like a bear," said Willow.

"Yeah," she said almost sarcastically. "Sure. Like a bear that can run faster than a horse over long distances. A bear that if you shoot it at point blank range, you'll only piss it off."

"So, nothing like a bear."

"Not even remotely. They're like nothing like you've ever seen. And I would know, Will. I've seen things that defy all manner of explanation. Spirits moving in graveyards. Homes that cannot be entered for fear they will eat their occupants. Women with wings who drink the blood of the innocent. Terrors that put at a slant the straight nature of all human reckoning. And each and every one of those I would rather face than a man who has become the beast living inside him."

"How many are there," he asked, wondering at the odds stacked against them should things go to shit.

"There are four brothers—the Brohms. The McKennys are more a clan than a family. I do not know their number, though it's greater, certainly."

"How many could we handle, say if they decide to turn?"

Carolina shook her head. "You must hear me

on this, Will. Hear it and keep it close. Make sure your brothers know, too – one is too great a force."

By the time they arrived at Les Pauvres l' atterrissage, the moon had risen high above them, swinging along the sky like a yellow sickle among heavy blue-gray clouds that promised rain. The wood-yard shack leaned against the landscape cold and lonely in the moonlight. Just beyond the meager wharf, the waters of the Missouri were black, rimmed at the banks with thin, glimmering slats of ice only one warm morning away from drifting down the river.

Carolina pulled a leaflet from her coat and held it up, reading the dark letters on the shining paper by the light of the moon.

"What's that?" asked Ellery.

"Riverboat schedule." She looked up and set her knuckles against the horizon and measuring by the width of hand-spans to approximate the hour, counted until her hand reached the moon. She put the sheet away, satisfied. "We're right on time."

They dismounted and brought their horses to the edge of the river, where their mounts drank, nose deep. Not long after, from down the length of the river, there came the shrill cry of a steamboat whistle.

They walked their ponies single file to the wharf to wait.

The steamboat came around a bend, all lit up by lanterns strung along the prow, which gave it a ghostly quality, its side paddles chewing up the river with a *whop-whop-whop*, churning toward them. The whistle shrieked again, cutting through the empty night. For some reason, that banshee scream mixed with the slow crawl of the boat gave Willow a terrible sense of dread.

"There she is," said Carolina. "*The White Rose*. She's a grand one, boys. We're lucky it's her. She'll take us by St. Louis and then all the way along the Kansas to our destination."

Willow took no comfort in the happiness in Carolina's voice. He watched the steamer glide toward them, reversing her paddles to slow her looming approach.

"Something bothering you, brother?" Ashley's voice was low, probing.

"Just worried about mother on the farm alone," he lied.

THE LITTLE
KANSAS BARONY

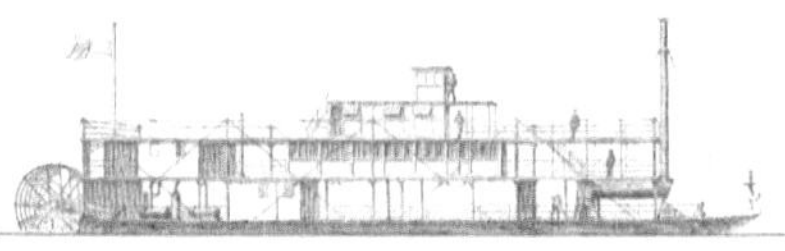

CHAPTER EIGHT

ABOARD THE STEAMER
WHITE ROSE,
LES PAUVRES L' ATTERRISSAGE
MISSOURI RIVER

The *White Rose* was a grand lady of a boat, much better than the rusty bucket that had carried Ashley down the river a few nights prior. They loaded onto the vessel, letting their horses be loaded into the lower deck where they would be fed and watered. Ashley was quite pleased with the boat. With her white paint and shiny black side-paddle wheels lapping up the dark waters of the Missouri to back out into the middle of the river, then turning about graceful as you please before the pilot set the wheels to churn against the flow. Six tall steam stacks, each flowered at the top, billowed steam near white as the paint on the three decks, stacked in fashion that gave the whole center of the boat the figure of a layer cake. A grand saloon was set at the bottom, just below the cabin and sun decks. Stained glass lanterns, shaded blue, glowed brightly where they hung upon silver trim hooks. The saloon windows were stained glass too, a shade of gold that when taken into view along with the silver-trimmed entryway of the saloon, made Ashley think that if heaven it existed, it would look just like this.

Carolina, with Will close at her side, led the brothers into the saloon. The two seemed to seeming to be getting along famously. She spoke to a somber-looking night attendant, inquiring about cabins for each of them. They would be taking this boat west, where the Kansas split from the Missouri.

Cabin rooms acquired, they made their way to the grand saloon. If the *White Rose* could be considered grand and fancy, the inside of the saloon was a marvel. The wooden floor was covered by large, thick carpets of black and gold and cream. There were tables everywhere, though not enough people to fill their number, and a large marble bar thirty feet long if it was an inch. Behind the bar was a red-haired woman, dressed sharp and professional in a fine black suit, mixing a drink for a slumped figure who had clearly seen better days. And just behind her, running the full length of the saloon were silver mirrors framed in black. At the far end of the steamer a water cooler stood stately as a monarch, three feet high, lacquered red, gleaming beside gilded water cups.

Carolina and Willow retired to the cabins, while Ashley and Ellery decided to have a drink, maybe join a game of poker being had among a trio of men smoking cigars.

They headed to the bar, ordered whiskeys. The busy bartender assured them she would pour for them shortly. While they waited, Ashley asked his younger brother if he knew the game of poker.

Ellery laughed. "You think you're the only one mother taught how to play table games?"

"That isn't a table game with mother," said Ashley, nodded his head at the trio of smoking gamblers. "We'll be playing for real money with what looks like a passel of peacocks."

"Peacocks?"

"Men of high leisure. Deep pockets. More money than sense."

"How do you know they aren't professional gamblers?"

"You've got a lot to learn, hayseed." He jokingly shoved his brother with a shoulder.

Ellery, thick as an oak, didn't move. "No, really. How can you tell?"

The bartender set their drinks atop the marble bar. Ashley paid her and waited for her to go back to the slumped man, who, despite the troubles clearly piled on his life, asked for more whiskey to go with them.

"Well, they're loose with how they hold their cards. They're playing with paper money and coin, not chips. And they're all pulling from the top of the deck without a dedicated dealer, and not a one of them watching when the other does it."

"Maybe they just trust each other."

Ashley shot his whiskey and clapped his brother on his meaty shoulder. "They do. Meaning, not a single gambler among them."

Ellery went to shoot his whiskey, but Ashley took his wrist. "Hold on," he said. He took the glass, dipped a few fingers, and dabbed the liquid on his neck and face.

"Hey, that was mine," said Ellery.

"Still is you big baby," said Ashley, handing the glass back to his brother. "Now listen. Here's how we play this. I've been drinking for the last three hours, and you're my concerned brother who is going to tell me that I should not get involved in another poker game. Say I'm tired and that I should go to bed before I lose my shirt."

Ellery furrowed his brow. "But you're not. You haven't."

"Right. . . But they don't know that."

Understanding, Ellery's face flattened in annoyance. "You're gonna grift 'em."

"No. *We* are going peacock hunting."

"Ashley—"

"It'll be fun. And call me Daniel Woodborough. I am the wayward son of a wealthy landowner, wasting our father's fortune up and down the river."

Ellery smiled big. "Well, that depiction is mostly true."

"You are not funny, smart-ass."

"Better to be unfunny than funny-looking like you."

Ashley couldn't help but smile, frustrated. It must have happened while he was gone. Ellery had become clever and sharp, his charm matching his size. Ellery had truly grown up. Become confident in both the power of his hands and his mind.

Even though Ashley was smiling, he felt regret, all at once delighted to meet the man his brother had become while missing the boy he had once been.

"Well," said Ellery, "I suppose it could be for a bit of fun. So, you're Daniel—"

"No," said Ashley. "I changed my mind. I don't think we'll gamble with those peacocks. I don't think I should get you involved with any of that."

"You think I can't do it," said Ellery, offended.

Ashley gave Ellery his full, earnest appraisal.

"I think you can do anything, brother. But this scheme reminded me of the last time I did it, six months ago with a fella named Rich Tuddle. We won for a while, then they saw through the grift. Shot at me with their pistols and missed. Then shot at Rich and didn't."

All the playfulness melted from Ellery's face, stealing the vision of the boy entirely, leaving only the man. "Aw, hell," he said. "Willow said you were in a low place when he found you, but we had no idea."

"St. Louis was all I wanted, until I got enough of it." Ashley looked over at the table of the gamblers, smoking their cigars and laughing like a pack of fools ready to be swindled. "I was stupid to leave home the way I did. Selfish. Breaking the hearts of the people I loved for the sake of what?" he asked himself. "For fucking what."

Ellery opened his mouth, but nothing came out.

Ashley shook his head. "Come on. Let's get some rest before tomorrow. This trip ain't that long, and I got a feeling we'll need all the rest we can get by its end."

They left, walking back out onto the deck of the *White Rose* together, and when he saw the blue lamps and gold windows and silver trim over all the wood, it didn't look like heaven at all. It just looked like a goddamn saloon.

That night, Willow did not sleep easy inside of his passenger cabin. He dreamed strange dreams, awoke lathered in a sweat, saw haunting faces in the shadows of trees rolling by outside his window. He lit an oil lamp, checked his pocket watch.

3:21 a.m.

If he'd had a bad dream, he couldn't remember it. But it certainly felt like it. Changing the damp bed sheets, he tried to go back to sleep. He closed his eyes and took a deep breath, immediately sat up and said, "There just ain't no way."

Not much caring for the long, drawn faces in the shadows along the riverbank, he dressed, washed his face, and stepped out onto the cabin deck. The clouds had rolled away, and the moon drifted lonely and pale through the blue-black night. The stars twinkled brightly. Bullfrogs, loud enough to be heard over the churning of the paddle wheels, groaned like displeased kings from muddy riverbank thrones. Smoke and cedar ruled all other smells.

He thought of his mother—alone, widowed, removed from all her sons. He never should have left. Watching the river go by, he leaned his elbows on the deck railing and tried to reason for himself how so much had happened so quickly. Life was moving faster than he liked, the changes coming on faster and faster, always unpredictable. And though he was surrounded by a hundred people and more in the cabins around him, Willow felt very alone. Very far from home.

From the corner of his vision, he saw light coming from under Carolina's cabin door. Shadows moved through the light cast upon the deck floor. It would be ungentlemanly to call on her at this hour. Rude. Unseemly. His mother would have chided him. Still.

Still.

He'd gotten on so well with her that he found himself wanting to talk to her. Know more about her. She was intelligent, sharp-tongued, worldly in a way he had never been. It was his want to hear her voice, and his desperate loneliness, that sent him to her door and lifting his hand to knock.

He paused. Reconsidered.

Then, knocked.

"Who is it?" came her voice from behind the door.

"Uhm. Willow Sutliff," he said, feeling like an idiot for using his whole name.

"Just a moment." There was a muffled shuffling. Steps coming close. Carolina opened the door holding an oil lamp, her other arm pinching a floral silk robe around her ample girth. Her brown ponytail hung over one shoulder, and though it was early, her eyes looked fresh. "Yes, Willow?"

"I. . . couldn't sleep. Saw your light," he said. "I'm sorry to pester."

The roundness of her cheeks lifted as she smiled. "No, it's quite alright. Sleep and I have never been close companions. It's cold though. Would you like to come inside?" And stepping back, she opened her shoulder to allow him entry.

His thoughts of impropriety suddenly cast aside by her open invitation, Willow stepped into the room nearly identical to his own. There were books strewn about the bed sheets, their titles printed in words he did not know, and a small set of reading glasses, neatly folded.

"Please," she said, inviting. "Won't you sit down?"

He did, sitting in the chair next to the window.

"Bad dreams?" she asked. "Nerves?"

Willow looked to the books on the bed, then to the sable carpet upon the floor. "Strange dreams. Worries."

He watched her as she passed by, sat on the bed, and crossed one milk-pale knee over the other. She slid the robe to cover her knees. "You're in a strange place. And I'm guessing you miss your mother," she said.

"Yes, ma'am."

"Ma'am might be all well and good for your

mother and for old ladies. Please, call me Carolina."

Willow nodded, lacing and unlacing at the fingers, his eyes wandering the cabin. "Okay."

"I want to tell you something Leigh told me last night as we were. . . preparing your father for burial."

The words painted a portrait in his mind that he did not wish to see, so he threw the thought of his father's corpse away and once again found her eyes.

"She told me that of all her sons, you were the one she worried about the least when it came to working and tending, being responsible. You do the right thing, time and time again. Ashley was too wild to tame. Ellery too young and jovial to yet know the dangers of the world. But you, she never had to worry about. Your father felt the same way. They knew they didn't have to worry about you, because you were always so worried about everything else."

It was true. He worried all the time, was always anxious about how his actions would affect others. "I am worried about her," he said, too softly. The words sounding unmanly in his ears.

"She knew you would be. But your mother is strong, and more than capable of bearing all she needs to bear. There is a great deal you don't know about her, her youth. Life before you and your brothers. And that is the way she would have it, so I will not break the promise I have made her. Still, as one of her oldest friends, I can tell you that she is a survivor, Willow. A woman who has seen terrible things and stood firm in the face of their terror. Your father enhanced those qualities, and even though he is gone, the woman she has become remains—magnified."

"She is. . . a remarkable woman," said Willow.

Carolina leaned forward, placing a comforting hand over his. "Singular." Her voice was soft, gentle. Kind in a way that utterly betrayed the sharpness of her wit. The way she spoke made Willow feel drawn to her in a way he had never been drawn to other women. Prettier women, younger. But looking at her now, in the golden yellow lamp glow, all of the things he'd been told he'd long after in other women, he found in her. She was older than him by fifteen years at least, and she didn't wear the fancy makeup or perfume the town ladies did. There was a strangeness to her proportion that took the features some might consider flaws—the way she looked, the way she acted, the way she talked—and transformed her into a sight to behold...

"Willow?" she asked, her eyes questioning. "What's wrong?"

"Uhm." He worried about what to say,

though he knew he had to say it. "Daddy. . . he used to say you should always be honest with a woman. Never mince words."

"I don't understand," she said. "Have you been dishonest with me?"

"Ms. Ellison—Carolina—I believe I would like to. . ."

Her eyes widened, and her mouth formed into a little 'o.' "Oh, Willow, wait just—"

"I believe I would like to kiss you, ma'am."

The words spoken, his worries blossomed to life as she slid her soft hand from his and shook her head. "You don't want to kiss me, Will. You want to kiss someone, and I'm here. You're over-wrought with grief and loss, and you, like all men, are looking for a good feeling to make you forget the bad one."

Willow thought to protest, tell her that wasn't the case at all, but she stood up, stepped away. "I am sorry, Willow, but no," she said. "No." Even her rejection was kind, delicate, prac-ticed. "I think you are a wonderful young man. I enjoy your company and your straight way of. . . saying your mind. But there are things we can be for each other and certain things we are not meant to be."

Part of him had expected this response. *Of course*, he thought. Why would a woman such as she want to kiss a man like him? And so, he stood up and, gathering his dignity in the hands of his manners, said, "You're right. I'm sorry to have been so forward. We barely know one another, and you're right. Of course you're right. I'm just tired. . . feeling poorly, and my thinking. . ." He put up a hand in apology, looked away. "I'll go back to my cabin, try to rest."

"Will—"

He was already opening the door, not quite catching what she said after his name. A thought crossed his mind. He stopped and turned back, keeping his eyes low. "If we could keep this between the two of us, I would be much obliged." He feigned a laugh. "If Ashley or Ellery—"

"Naturally," she said. "A passing moment between new friends. Nothing else."

He nodded again, feeling a fool, and exited her cabin.

It was only when he reached the cabin deck that he felt his heart racing, his sweat chilled by the cold early morning air. "So stupid," he whispered. "So fucking stupid."

He was too mad to sleep. His blood too hot with embarrassment. His pocket watch showed just past four. The sun would be cutting the twilight soon, and he figured on a luxury steamer like this, he'd be able to order himself some coffee and get started with the day. Start fresh. Move forward. Try to forget the last thirty minutes had ever happened.

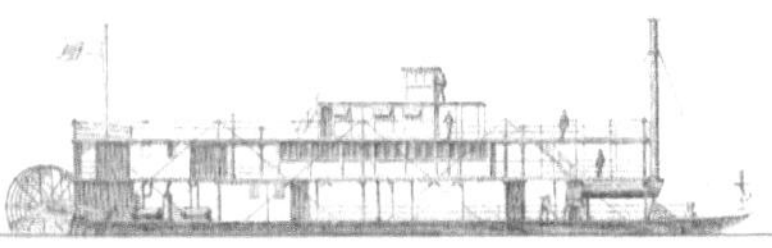

CHAPTER NINE

ABOARD THE STEAMER *WHITE ROSE*, ST. LOUIS MISSOURI RIVER

Ashley was having himself a fine morning smoke as the morning dimpled the black waters with silver light, like some great giant had thrown a thousand coins onto the surface. Time strolled by. The sun rose higher, turning the coins red and every ripple of the river gold. Ashley smoked, watching it all, wondering why he had wasted so many nights in saloons where grimy oil lamps and lanterns threw long shadows over cards and chips and cold-eyed gamblers looking to rob him blind or cut his throat. In those places had been a hundred faceless dealers who would always call him 'Mr. Sutliff,' but whenever he returned after an absence, not a one of them remembered his name.

Carolina found him up there and told him she was headed into the city to gather her brother and his companion.

"The hotel where he's staying is none-too-far from here, so no need in us all unloading," she had said.

Ashley offered to escort her, but the look on her face told him her precise thoughts on needing a man to help her get to where she was going. She had left him to his cigarettes and crisp Missouri air. There were other people on the deck, and they came and went, their conversations mostly about the people or places they had traveled to visit. He listened for a little while, smoking, until hunger came and he made his way down the promenade toward the saloon.

Inside, he found the place packed with travelers of all sorts, Creoles and freemen and ladies looking fresh and pretty as the morning. What he did not expect to spy was Willow's long, skinny form leaning on the marble bar, looking bleary-eyed and flushed red as a candied apple.

He strode over to find him peering off into nothing, one hand curled around a whiskey glass.

"Well, hello there, dear brother," said Ashley, as if they had not seen each other in years. "Either you're drunk or the morning disagrees with you more than I remember."

Willow turned to him, sneered. "You've had

your fill, I am certain," he slurred, turning the word *am* into *ham*. "Now let me have mine."

Ashley nearly laughed out loud. "Well, what in the hell happened to you?"

Willow squinted. "I was born a worrier," he said, his tone heavy with self-rebuke.

"Do what—"

"And you," he said, all breathy and melodramatic with drink, "you never worry about anything. But what have you ever had to fear." His eyes suddenly turned glassy as he swayed slightly. "You, first-born, free of care and responsibility, becoming a goddamned gambler while the rest of us became who we were supposed to be!"

Ashley raised his palms to gesture for his brother to lower his volume.

"Hey," cried a man sitting with a young lady and a young child at a nearby table. "Take that drunk out of here. Some people are trying to eat their breakfast!"

"Will, I don't know what is going on—"

"You *never* know what the hell is going on because you're always off doing whatever you want. You're so goddamn shitting focused on. . . focused on. . ."

"Goddamn shitting?" asked Ashley, genuinely confused. "Brother, right now I'm just focused on getting you out of here without—"

"Without *what*?" The last word was so loud

that it cracked the low hum of the crowd. "Without making a mistake? Without soiling the family name?" He took an unsteady step toward Ashley, leaning close. "I suppose you could tell me, brother, is this what it looks like? That staining you have done so well."

And there it was.

Ashley felt a lump form in his throat, all the glory of the morning sun forgotten and all the years inside the saloons remembered. "I am—"

"I said get that drunk out of here."

Ashley peered around Willow to see the man rising from his chair. He was wearing a fine suit, his black hair shiny as wet crow feathers. He had a little mustache and lime green eyes that caught the light.

"Do it," the man said. "Or I will."

Ashley felt all the tension in his hands, his shoulders and between himself and his brother, all of it ready to uncoil. "Mister, I am trying to..."

Willow leaned closer to Ashley. His expression flattened, eyes going cold. "Mother says I mus love you, but I do not like you at all, big brother."

The words, like the head of the shovel they'd used to dig their father's grave, slammed down into Ashley's heart and scooped out a piece of him, leaving a hollow place in his chest. It made him want to apologize. Made him want to say anything that would restore the admiration that had shined in Willow's eyes when they were boys. They had been so close. Had two years away stretched such a distance between them?

Ashley searched his eyes for the love of the boy he had once known. But he didn't find it. All he found was the widening anger, and the dilation of a pupil just after a decision is made and just before the action is taken.

Willow turned on his hip and from out of nowhere Ashley's vision went white with pain. A gasp shot through the room, then it fell silent as a church. Ashley reached up, dabbed at his eyebrow where he felt the warm, stinging gap along the thin hairline.

From the new hollow in his heart came a red burning anger. He flew into Willow, taking him at the waist as he had done so many men like him before. And he slipped a leg around his brother's calf, and they fell together, Ashley on top. They had wrestled many times as boys, never once with the intent to do true harm, but this was different. Willow had swung and with a single strike changed the whole sum of their history.

Ashley pressed his advantage, smothering his brother's face with his hands, slapping away his long reach. Then, gripping Willow's throat, Ashly raised a hand, balling his fingers into a fist, but before he could strike the world went white again, and then black and suddenly he was on his back.

The suited man from the table stood over him, fists cocked, smiling. "I said knock that shit—"

A huge fist lanced out, taking the man right in the mouth. He went tumbling back, a hot spray of blood streaming from his nose.

The man hit the floor, and did not move.

Ashley tilted his head at the figure standing over him.

There stood Ellery, looking mean as a bull and only half its size. Eyes wide, filled with malice.

Ashley knew that look. "Ellery," he said. "Wait—"

But Ellery stepped over him and past Willow, stalking toward the unconscious man.

Ashley hollered, "Ellery!"

The youngest Sutliff leaned over the fallen man, gripped him by the collar, and hit him so hard that teeth sprayed all over the fine steamer carpet.

"Daddy!" the little girl at the table screamed.

"Howard!" the mother howled.

Ellery, blind and deaf, all bull in his rage, struck the man again.

"Will," cried Ashley, scrambling to his feet. "He's gonna kill 'im"

Willow, seemingly forgetting his rage toward

Ashley, drunkenly scrambled to his feet, almost falling over. They charged and collided with Ellery at the same time, spilling over one of the fine tables in a mess of tangled limbs, shattering plates, and shining silverware.

Ellery was up faster than the other two and looked to Ashley, the rage inside him melting to betrayal. "Why are you hittin' me? I was helping!"

Ashley put up his hands. "Goddamn it, Ellery. You can't be—"

"What in the name of Christ Almighty is going on in here!" came a voice, rolling deep and loud as a thunderstorm.

The Sutliff brothers, all three, snapped their eyes over to the open saloon doors.

Carolina Ellison stood there bookended by two men Ashley did not know. To her left was a tall youth, slender faced and blue eyed. On the right was black-bearded man tall as Ellery, bald as a boiled egg, and wearing a frock coat that a smaller man might have used for a tent.

"Uh," said Ashley, slowly pushing to his feet. "Hello there. You must be Hezekiah Ellison. I'm Ashley Sutliff and, uh, these two here are my brothers. Willow and Ellery."

The big man looked to Carolina. "You're kidding me."

Carolina put her hands on her hips, shaking

her head. "I wish I was, brother." She pursed her lips. "I wish I was."

Until the end of his days, Willow Sutliff would remember the first time he saw Hezekiah Ellison and the fire in those eyes. The force. The belief.

Hezekiah had the hands of a miner and the shoulders of an ox, and he carried a big pistol holstered to a thigh thick as a ham, but it wasn't his size that stopped Willow from waylaying his brother; it was those eyes. They were like Carolina's, but brighter, catching the light in such a way to reveal a burning intelligence. Eyes that would not brook an argument. The eyes of a prophet living in perpetual revelation.

The other man was a picket fence of a figure, spindly, dark-haired with sunken-cheeks and a viper's resting smile. He wore a black suit matched by a black tie that sliced a straight line through his white shirt

"Well, it's a damn mess you've brought me," said Hezekiah to his sister.

Carolina looked at Willow, disappointment in her eyes. "I told you," she said. "They're young. Inexperienced."

"Send 'em on home, eh?" said the undertaker-looking fellow. "These boys can't even get along with each other. Can't figure they'll make things better if tensions get high in Kansas."

"Maybe I will," said Hezekiah, his tone gruff. He turned back to the three brothers standing over the bleeding man. "You three," he snapped. "Get your damn asses—"

"Who is making trouble on my boat," barked a voice, and a man stalked into the saloon with a rifle in his hands. His blue coat was riveted shut with brass buttons, and he glared around with a face not even a mother could love.

It was the damndest thing Willow Sutliff had ever seen: Hezekiah Ellison painted a smile on his face, the light in his eyes seemed to shift brighter, and the seriousness of his manner suddenly became a mask of charm. "Why, that must be Captain Chandler Prouleux, the famous river man who I have heard so much about on my way down the Ohio!"

By the look on his face, the way he smirked at the words, Captain Prouleux was a man deeply in love with the story of himself. Hezekiah's words had knocked all the fury out of his demeanor. "I am he, sir."

Hezekiah put up his hands, playing the role of a fanatic meeting an idol. "Captain of the *White Rose*, fair and honorable in all deals, protector of female virtue, and agent of justice in all matters taking place on his boat. A darling beauty of a boat, if I may say so, Captain." He didn't even take a breath. "And I *do*—I say it openly and honestly, before holy God and all these witnesses to the minor scuffle and misunderstanding that has taken place in this divine saloon of unmatched quality. Why the glass and the lanterns, Captain. The marble of the bar, the silver mirrors all around. It is a shame that my nephew here was come upon by one of his. . ." Hezekiah put a big arm around the captain's shoulder, whispered something behind his hand that Willow could not hear.

The captain's mouth went from a grim line to an 'o' of sudden understanding.

"Now," said Hezekiah, snapping his gaze down at the boatman's rifle. "Is this. . . ? Tell me this is Rosemary."

The captain smiled, damn near blushed. "Certainly is."

"Why, sister," said Hezekiah, though he now had the whole crowd enraptured, "this is the one. The custom St. Louis rifle that made the two-hundred–yard shot that struck the bell of the steamer *Jeffers Ford*."

"Oh, this is the man who made that shot?" said Carolina, flourishing with a hand that had drawn out a silk handkerchief.

Captain Prouleux sniffed, the braggart blooming out of him. "It was closer to two-seventy-five, as I recall."

"Now, please, Captain," Hezekiah said, "let me pay for the damages my men have made to the table—"

"And my goddamn face." The suited man was standing now, both eyes puffing red, nose busted.

Hezekiah put up a plaintiff hand. "Absolutely, sir. My nephews are prone to violence due to their horrific upbringing, all of them eunuchs, nary a one with a lick of sense that reasonable men bear within themselves."

"A do what now," said Ellery.

"I am many things," Ashley began, "but I am not a—

"Man capable of knowing when to behave," Hezekiah said, flaring the fire in his eyes at them again, "or when to tussle. It is my poor fortune, Captain. I am loath to bring them with me on my business in Kansas on this fine steamer of yours. I assure you. Damages will be paid, and no future incident will occur." His tone softened again, becoming charming. Liquid. "Provide us the fairness and grace that has made me such a fan of yours."

Captain Prouleux rubbed his pocked chin, thinking it over. "Not another incident?"

"I can assure you."

"Then on your word, I'll allow it."

Willow, near spellbound by Hezekiah's act, shook his head.

Hezekiah walked over to him, all that social grace diminished with each step. The big man leaned in close. "You look to be the drunkest man

I ever saw, and that makes me think you're the fuse that lit this damn powder keg."

Willow thought a moment, his mind still hazy from the whiskey. "It is more complicated than that."

Hezekiah sneered. "Only to a simple mind." He placed a heavy paw on Willow's shoulder. "This is my friend and agent, Mr. Julius Stephens," he said gesturing to the tall, black suited man who had entered the room with him. "He will see you to your cabin. There you will sober up." He squeezed so hard that the fingers near touched bone. "If I didn't know and so deeply respect your parents, I'd have chucked you over the side of this boat. Let you drown if too drunk or swim home if you weren't. Your parents I know. You, I do not. Don't ever put me in that position again."

"I didn't mean—"

Hezekiah was having none of it. "Go sober up, spud. We'll make proper introductions then. More talking will only agitate me further."

Will, flush with anger and drink and embarrassment, caught Carolina's disappointed gaze and, gritting his teeth, did as Hezekiah said.

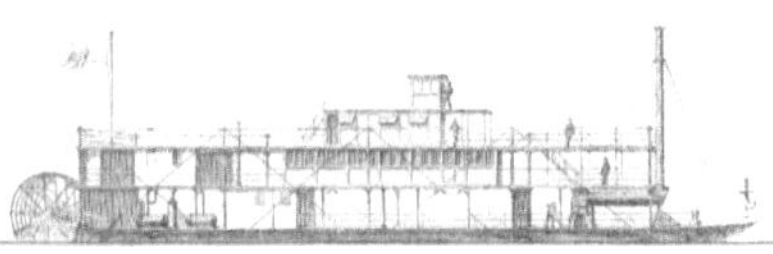

CHAPTER TEN

ABOARD THE STEAMER
WHITE ROSE,
MISSOURI RIVER JUNCTION
SMOKEY HILL RIVER CUTOFF

A shley ate breakfast with Ellery who, from time to time, looked over at the man he had pummeled.

"Leave it," said Ashley, forking a pile of eggs into his mouth. "Eat your beefcakes."

"Goddamn son of a bitch," said Ellery. He pressed his knife through the beefcake, stabbed it with his fork, but didn't eat. "Gettin' involved like that."

"Wasn't his fault. I shouldn't have let things get so far with Will. I should have been smarter than to talk to him that way when he was liquored up." The steam had been building between them for a long time, for longer than the two years Ashley was in St. Louis. He supposed all brothers kept a ledger of slights and frustrations inside their minds at all times. The bill of their conflict had come due, hastened by the whiskey.

"And that Ellison, talking to Will the way he did, sending him to his cabin like a whipped pup," Ellery said. "I should have twisted his head off for that. And that other fella with him, Julius Stephens or whatever his name is."

"That was the name Ellison gave. Look, it was a bad introduction, and we screwed up."

Ellery looked up, wounded. "I didn't do anything wrong."

Ashley shook his head. "Brother, you can't walk into a saloon filled with normal, nice folks and near beat a man to death. . . in front of his family no less."

"What was I to think? I come in here, see that fella whoopin' on y'all—"

"Whoa," said Ashley. "Nobody was whooping me."

Ellery's eyes half-closed, his lips pursed.

Ashley laughed. "I am amazed," he said.

"At what?"

"You've grown into something, you know? More than just your size; you've developed a real personality. It's good to see."

Ellery flashed his teeth, slanting his still too-boyish grin. "Two years away and I find you still much the same, big brother. Impatient. At odds with Willow. Well, actually. . ." He rubbed his chin, looking up to the ceiling as he considered a point. "I think one thing has changed. You are now the second best-looking Sutliff."

"What a goddamn smart-ass you have become."

Slowly, the boyish grin slipped from Ellery's face. He slid his tongue across his teeth, took a deep breath.

For as long as Ellery had been able to speak, Ashley knew the gesture. His brother was about to ask a question he thought was very serious. To finally unload something that had been on his mind. This was Ellery's great social tell. It always had been, and it always would be.

"What are we doing here, Ashley?" asked Ellery.

There it was.

"Right now? We're having breakfast."

Ellery shook his head. "You know what I mean."

"We're doing exactly what we're supposed to be doing. Mother says go, we ask how far. She tells us to jump, we ask how high. . ."

"And if mother says it's Christmas in July, you better hang your stocking because Santa Claus is coming to town," finished Ellery. It was an old saying their father had said many times in jest at the dinner table, and in rebuke when the boys had disobeyed. "I'm serious, brother. What the hell are we doing with these strange people, headed to a strange place. We should be at home, working."

Ashley sucked his teeth. "Daddy told me a promise was made to help these people with whatever they need, and what they need is for us to protect them while they go about whatever this strange business is. So that's what we're gonna do. It falls to us to repay the debt."

"Hell, we've got money. Why, I sold six horses just the other week, and—"

"Not all debts work that way, El. It's not what we owe but the promise we made. People get caught up in what's owed. Believe me, as a man who has owed a great deal. They get violent over debts incurred and those never to be repaid. But they aren't mad about the money. Money comes, goes. The hurt is the broken promise. The disrespect."

Ellery leaned an elbow on the table, setting his chin against his big fist. "Learned that as a gambler, did you?"

"No," said Ashley, wounded, but not so much by the words as by the remembering of the lesson. "Daddy."

Ellery let out a long, almost mournful, "Mmm."

Ashley looked to his brother. "I am more than just a gambler, little brother. Who I am is greater than the two years I was in St. Louis. I didn't leave because I hated home. I left because. . . because. . .”

"Because home wasn't good enough. I get it.”

"No,” snapped Ashley, suddenly frustrated. "I left because there is an ache inside of me. A need. When I see the farm, I don't see a place I despise. I see all the memories made there, just as you do. But when I look beyond it—past the ringlet of trees and the river and where the river goes— well, there I see a way to places I can find. . . I dunno. . . find who I am supposed to be.”

"Not just the son of a hog farmer?”

Ashley tsked. "No goddamn it. Well, I mean, yes.” He was suddenly flustered. "Daddy was more than a hog farmer. He had a life before us, just like mother did. And these people, Hezekiah and Carolina, they came looking for him when they needed help. Don't you want to know why that was? Don't you want to know what was expected of him by such strange folk, before sickness took him? Wouldn't you be willing to wager your whole life on the prospect of accomplishing that which Daddy, the most capable man you have ever known, was entrusted?”

Ellery leaned back, letting his back hit the shoulders of the chair. "So, you want to do what Daddy couldn't?”

The question hit Ashley like a sledgehammer blow. Ellery had missed the entire point. "No,” he said. "I want to do something *for* him. And for mother."

"Even if it involves taking on these men who can supposedly, miraculously"—he flourished a hand in the air like a magician conjuring a silk scarf from his sleeve—"change their very shape from man to beast? And who kill quick and easy as any living predator?"

"Yes," said Ashley, as serious as he got. "I mean to make good on my promise. No matter the circumstance. No matter the cost."

Ellery tilted his head to one side, then the other. Pursed his lips and took a sip of his coffee. "Well, I'm with you, big brother. With you all the way."

The fever of Willow's dreams broke with the shrill cry of the *White Rose* getting up her full steam, announcing to God and the river and the whole of St. Louis that she was putting out. Outside his window, the sky was bruised with deep purple clouds and the dying yellow of the sun setting amid their downy sheen. The river, bronzed by the fading light, was lined with other steamers. Some were big and fancy, their names painted proudly on their pilot houses, but not a single one as grand as the *White Rose*. His was head aching something awful and his throat dry as a bag of sand, and remembered the argument with Ashley, the fight, and all the rest. Most of all he remembered the look on Carolina's face. The disappointment.

He threw the sheets back, went to the little water basin near his bed, and washed his face and hair. He rinsed his mouth with what water was left and then looked at himself in the shaving mirror. Small as it was, he could see all the hell he'd done to himself.

"What would Daddy say?" he asked himself, feeling the disapproval all the way from Heaven. And Willow Sutliff, at that moment, and for all the moments that were left in his life, made a vow to never touch whiskey again.

He dressed himself, combed his hair, and went out onto the passenger deck to Carolina's room. He would arrive, knock, apologize.

Willow did the first two, but after he got no answer, he went all over the boat—from sun deck to Texas deck to boiler deck—seeking out Carolina. But there was no sign of her or her brother—or, for that matter, his own. He wondered if maybe they had all disembarked the *White Rose*, perhaps left him behind for his bad behavior. Wandering the steamer, he began to ask around, person to person, to see if anyone knew where his companions had gone. After questioning a few passengers on the hurricane deck, he approached a one-eyed man, wearing a white eye-patch and a fine blue suit adorned with a single silver pin on his lapel. At first Will thought it was a law badge of some kind, but it wasn't. It was simply engraved with the number 1. The man grinned at him with a slanted smile. "I seen 'em," he said. Then spat over the side of the boat, turned, and pointed up to the big square pilot house. He thanked the man, then turned to go.

The man called to him. "You the one got blown-out drunk this morning?"

Willow gave him a stare.

"Hey, now, young'un, no need to be giving me that look. I just heard about it over lunch. Thought maybe I'd help you steer clear of the drink. You know, if it's a demon to you. Used to own me too."

Willow sighed. "I am not a drunk."

"Yeah." The man cracked that smile of his. "Sure. In any case, you get a thirst, come and find me. Name's Chelsea Vermillion. Friends and old rivals call me Red." There was a sincerity there, a veteran kindness that seemed well worn and eagerly practiced. "Thanks," said Willow, and giving the man no more mind than that, he rushed up the decks toward the ornate pilot house. In his hurry, he blew past men and women and nearly knocked over three kids all walking like ducks in a row behind their mother, apologizing to each and every one fast as he could. He ricocheted from a corner to the stairwell rail, breathless, and raced up the steps.

The pilot house itself was square as a cracker box with its sharp edges and tall beams and fancy carved paneling and stained window glass frosted white, fancy as a lady's necklace. The pilot-house door was chestnut brown, halfway up its length the wood had been cut away and in the gap the carpenters had placed a big window, where on the colored glass, in gold letters it read, *White Rose*. From inside came voices. Then a man laughing.

Willow knocked.

"*Entrer*," bellowed a male voice. Willow opened the door. Captain Prouleux was sitting in a fancy leather chair, head thrown back, howling with glee.

The Ellisons, their companion, and his brothers were sitting on couches in a little area before a hearth, warm and cozy as a den. Set at the center of the wide, clear windows a little man dressed in overalls clutched portions of a great wheel, so big that half of it disappeared beneath the fine floorboards. He must have been the pilot, for he reached between cords, pulled a lever, and called down one of the brass-fitted voice pipes, saying, "That's enough, Mike. That's the steam we need." And beyond the pilot, through the window, the whole of the black Missouri stretched out like some dark serpent, frozen mid-slither by winter's chill.

"Captain Prouleux," said Ashley, snatching Will's attention from the vastness of the river. "This is my brother, Willow Sutliff. A consummate hand, the hardest working man you will find on either side of your beloved river."

Will found himself awful confused.

The captain regarded Will kindly. "Come on in, son," he said. "Mr. Ellison has told me all about your troubles with a bottle. And, though it was on my boat, I admit that I too have known the distemper of the drink a time or two. Come. Sit." He gestured to one of the couches, near Carolina Ellison.

Willow eyed Carolina. She gave him a curt smile, a stiff nod. And he went over to sit next to his brothers. Ellery grinned. Ashley was smiling too, but the intent in his eyes said clearly, "Play along."

"*Entrer*," said the captain, happy at the sound of it. "You know, Mr. Ellison, I have traveled this river for years and never once taken a ken to learning French. I suppose I should have, but a captain has other responsibilities. Other passions. Foremost, his lady." He lifted his hands, palm-up, gesturing at the grandeur of the pilot house. "But your talk is fine to listen to, sounding like one of them fancy Creole boys."

"My own life has required the picking up of certain dialects and the languages that house them," said Hezekiah. "And indeed, you have a fine steamer. Finest I've ever set foot upon. And I would know. I have traveled on the Ohio, the Mississippi, thousands of miles of river on dozens of boats. Yes, sir. The *White Rose* is the best." The big man reached into his coat and produced a leather pouch. He plucked out a big, acorn bowled pipe already packed with dark ribbons of tobacco. "Now," he said as a preamble between lighting the pipe with a freshly struck match and speaking. He puffed twice, bringing forth curls of sweet-smelling smoke. "As to my business at the junction. . ."

The captain shook his head. "I want to do you this favor, Mr. Ellison, but I am a steamboat captain, and that comes with responsibilities of getting passengers and freight to their destinations on time. Going down the Smoky Hill will delay us too much. Won't it, Mr. Mills," he called over to the little pilot at the wheel.

"Near half a day by my reckoning," said the pilot, keeping his eyes focused on the river.

"Ah, you see?" said the captain. "Comfort, safety, and timely course. These are the things I am known for, Mr. Ellison. And as a man who has traveled so many miles on steamers less grand than my girl, you must know, reputation is everything on this river. I cannot risk mine."

Hezekiah smoked for a moment, considering. "I am a man of means," he said. "Say I could compensate you for the half-day?"

Captain Prouleux shook his head. "Your money I could spend in a week. My boat's reputation would take months to recover."

Carolina straightened. "Captain, my brother and I have reputations, too. We chose your boat because we heard she is not only grander but faster than all other boats. What was it, Hezekiah? Eight big boilers on this fine steamboat? Captain, perhaps you could make up the time using that speed that has made you so famous. Or was I misinformed?"

The captain seemed to bristle. "Ma'am, this lady is a heller of a boat. Becomes a demon if I ask her to. However, running with that much push is not only dangerous but also expensive in both wood and the sweat of my stokers."

Ashley leaned forward and steepled his fingers beneath his chin. "Wouldn't it increase your reputation if you were to take this small detour and yet still make your destination on time? Wouldn't that gamble be worth the risk?"

"I do not play cards. I do not visit roulette wheels. And I have never bucked the tiger," said the captain, unmoved. "Gambling is for men who hate money, or who hate themselves so badly they cannot imagine living with anything or anyone but the thrill of risk. They are orphans or the sons of lesser men, in my experience."

Willow shot his eyes over to Ashley. Where he expected to find his brother flush with frustration, he found only a placid mask, a smooth and unperturbed poker face. It impressed him.

"So," said Hezekiah, pulling the pipe from his teeth, "it is a matter of time, money, and reputation that keeps you from helping. Not the fear that it would bring you close to the Little Kansas Barony."

The captain's smile melted off his face. "Careful, Mr. Ellison. I find you charming, but do not insult me."

Hezekiah waved his hand dismissively. "There is no insult intended, Captain. I assure you. I only know that the river trade has ebbed in that portion of the territory. There is a great amount of money waiting to be had for those willing to run their packet lines in those waters. Cotton, indigo, tobacco, all manner of freight aching to be sold on other portions of the Missouri. But the leaders of the Barony have choked the river, keeping men such as yourself from claiming the hundreds of thousands of dollars. A man in St. Louis told me that a packet company might make millions trolling the western portion of the river alone. . ."

"You're meeting with them?" asked the captain, a little tremor in his voice.

"I am," said Hezekiah.

Captain Prouleux scanned the group, thinking. "About opening the river?"

"Not primarily," said Hezekiah. "They've called me to help negotiate a land dispute. But I have their ear, Captain. Their trust. Imagine what a man might profit if he granted me a favor on my journey there. A man with a fast enough boat to get me there on time. Perhaps, in my gratitude, I would suggest to the barony that the Smoky Hill River trade should be reopened, made exclusive to just one packet company."

The captain rested back into his chair, running his fingers along his smooth cheeks. "It's dangerous. Risky."

"A gamble," said Ashley.

The captain smirked. "Not if I have an assurance. I'll tell you what, Mr. Man of Means, I will strike you a deal. I'll set you down at the junction, you deliver the river to my Flower Top Packet line exclusive, like you said. And should you fail, you'll be buying me another boat, one even grander than my *Rose*."

"Why," said Hezekiah calm, cool, smooth as the acorn bowl of his pipe, "that sounds like quite the investment."

Captain Prouleux's eyes flashed, his demeanor cold. "It's quite the goddamn risk."

It was the first time that Willow saw Hezekiah Ellison bring his smile to bear. In its shape, he saw the pure delight of victory. A negotiation won.

"That's not a no," said Hezekiah.

Captain Prouleux ran his tongue over his buttermilk teeth, looking them all over. Then, he extended a hand across the little space between himself and Hezekiah. "It's a yes," he said.

The two men shook.

That evening, the group of travelers dined in one of the little partitioned areas in the saloon. The table could seat ten but had been set with china sets for six. Hezekiah moved his own place setting so that he sat at the head of the table next to Will. He'd asked the captain for a private table, and Prouleux had agreed and called down to the boiler deck for the first mate to manifest the accommodations. Red wine and oysters on the half-shell were served. Will drank water and didn't touch the oysters. He decided to wait on the main course, which turned out to be roasted chicken, mashed potatoes, and purple carrots in a creamy mushroom sauce.

"Mr. Ellison," said Julius Stephens, clasping his glass of wine in a knobby hand. The man was all angles it seemed. "Believe now is a proper time to talk to these boys about what's to be expected."

"I believe you're right, Julius." Hezekiah set down his fork and knife, and laced his fingers into a dome above his plate.

"Probably not getting drunk and fighting each other," said Ellery, smirking with a cheek stuffed with potatoes.

Carolina laughed.

Ashley shook his head, slanting a look over at Willow.

Willow didn't like being made a joke of, but he let it go, seeing now how childish his actions had been. He wanted to do his mother proud, to prove himself as capable a man as his father would have wanted. "No, probably not," he said and looked directly at Carolina so that their eyes met. "About that. I, uhm, I apologize."

Carolina nodded, accepting the apology quietly between them.

"It's over and done with," said Hezekiah. "Before we talk about what's ahead, I wanted to give the three of you my sincere condolences for the loss of your father."

Willow felt a shadow fall over him, and he looked down the table to see that Ellison's unexpected words fell over his brothers with the same effect. Ashley sipped his wine. Ellery stopped cutting his steak.

"Thank you," said Willow.

"Well, don't thank me yet, slim," said Hezekiah, settling back into his chair. "See, your daddy was one of the bravest, most capable men I have ever known. There was a time when he and I were. . . in a way. . . you would not say enemies but certainly opponents. Carolina and I were mixed up in a bad situation with some bad people, along with your mother who—"

"Hezi," said Carolina sharply.

Hezekiah looked over to her.

She shook her head.

He nodded, continued. "Well, it all shook out in a way that got me and my sister here into the line of work that we do. I'm certain she has told you that we hire out to people who can assist us in our purpose. We're still young as a company, but we've already had our shining moments." He looked to his plate, a pall falling over his bright eyes. "And our tragedies and defeats and losses." He straightened again, producing his pipe from his coat. He lit it, smoked, continued. "The reason I say that is to tell you that your daddy was a part of those shining moments. He was capable in a way I suspect you do not know, because, as I recall, he never was the braggart. He was never the best at any one thing. Well. . . if timely meanness is a skill, then I suppose he was the master of that. Anyway, he wrote to me a time or two before his passing, so I know some about you."

He leveled his eyes at Ashley. "You'd be the oldest. A gambler." Then at Ellery. "Little Ellery is what he called you, but I can see that didn't last long. The ranch hand." Finally, at Willow. "And you, Willow. The rider. Now, none of you know who the fuck I am, other than what my sister has said, and she never says too much."

"She told us about the werewolves," said Ashley, interrupting. Always interrupting, thought Willow. "About the Brohms of the Little Kansas Barony, and the McKennys."

"Yeah," said Hezekiah, half-smiling. "Sure, you know the names of the families. But what Mr. Julius Stephens here was getting at, is that you need to know what's expected of you. Here's what I need you to understand." The man, wide as an oak, leaned his heavy countenance on them. "Do not say or do anything without my say so."

"Taking orders was never really my thing," said Ashley.

Willow looked over at his brother. "Could you just. . . for a minute, listen and not—"

Ashley shook his head. "Afraid not, little brother. Because this fella right here is hiding something, or outright lying to us." He kept his eyes pinned on Hezekiah. " My parents owe you, which is why we three are here. You know a bit about me, that much is certain, but hear this, Ellison: while I am a gambler of money, I rarely gamble with my life. And I hate waiting. I am not going to wait to get to Kansas for you to be straight with us. So," he said, eyes flaring, "cut the shit. Show your hand."

"Why you little prick," said Julius, his voice sharp.

"He wasn't talking to you," said Ellery, backing his brother's play.

The table fell quiet.

Hezekiah glared at Ashley.

Ashley glared right back.

Carolina sipped at her wine, looking bored.

And suddenly, what began as a respite dinner became overcrowded with tension. Poised for violence.

Julius Stephens slipped one hand below the table, eyeing Ashley the whole time. And he had slowed his breathing. Willow didn't like that subtle movement. Not one damn bit. And his instincts, mixed with the notion that this man might mean Ashley harm, took over. He drew his pistol fast as an unseen snake strikes from the high grass.

Julius's eyes went wide.

"Easy with those hands," said Willow, suddenly angrier than he could remember being in a very, very long time.

"Christ," said Carolina. "Could everyone just calm the fuck down?" She looked to her brother.

"Enough with the damn secrecy, Hezi. They deserve to know anyhow."

Hezekiah smirked, then his shoulders shook, and the big son of a bitch started laughing. "I swear to God. Ashley and Ellery have their mother's tongue, but it looks like all three of you have your daddy's meanness. Your speculation is fair. I am slow to trust. It is one of my many failings. But I suppose my sister is right, and, Ashley, you are keen to see my lack of transparency." He looked to Will, who was still holding Julius at gunpoint, and for a moment looked confused, as if Willow were the silliest man alive. "Son, you can put that away. Mr. Stephens is no threat to you."

Willow took in a slow breath, then holstered his revolver.

"Let me begin anew, yes? Bring you into the whole truth of the thing. The Brohms are a problem," said Hezekiah. "I've known them for several years. I admit that I've even worked to aid their purpose a time or two, because it aligned with my own. The McKennys, on the other hand, are simply trying to cut out a life for themselves in America, as so many others wish to do. As a matter of fact, I helped McKennys immigrate here, paid for the whole. . . pack, you might say, because I thought they would find refuge with those of their own kind. However, they did not agree with the way the Brohms run their little barony, and so the Brohms rejected them outright. Tensions have grown high. Blood has been spilled. And, because I know the leaders of both, I was asked to come and act as a mediator for their peace."

Ashley gave that unhappy laugh of his. "You aren't going to negotiate," he said. "You're going to ambush the Brohms."

Willow wasn't sure how Ashley had come to that conclusion. But before he could question, Carolina said, "Yes."

Hezekiah snapped his eyes over to her. "Maybe," he said.

"No," said Carolina, chiding. "Not maybe. Not if they did what the McKennys' said they did."

Hezekiah heard his sister and nodded. "Right."

"What did they do?" asked Ellery.

"The McKennys wrote to me, saying—"

"Christ, Hezi. Just get to the fucking point," said Carolina, and then leveled her eyes on Ellery. "They killed three McKennys who were caught hunting outside the pack line. One of whom was a child. Fourteen years old. Not too far from your age."

"Pack line?" asked Willow.

"Lycanthropes normally work in a collective mindset: an all-together-as-one mentality. The pack is each of them, and each of them the pack," said Hezekiah, crossing one leg over the other. "At least that's how it worked in their native countries for centuries. However, the Little Kansas Barony has broken with that tradition. These American werewolves run the four sections of their territory like self-made aristocrats, not unlike those goddamn piece-of-shit slavers of this country."

"Mr. Ellison is a proponent of abolition," piped up Julius Stephens, now smiling with both hands on the table. "As we all are."

"Goddamned fucking right," said Hezekiah, and he took a deep breath as if he were about to rush headlong into a tirade.

"Hezi," said Carolina. "The pack line. . ."

He shook his head and, with a wave of his hand, seemed to dissipate the fog of his anger. "The pack line is the pecking order. Who gets to hunt what and when and where. Well, the McKennys were starving, and so they went out to find something to eat. They were in their. . . true form, and the Brohms caught them bloody muzzled and red-handed."

"How'd they catch them?" asked Willow. "Seems like an awful big coincidence to know where the McKennys were located, and to do it in the middle of a hunt makes it seem. . ."

"Like a goddamn setup," said Ellery. "Brohms starve the McKennys, forcing them to break the pack line. . ."

Hezekiah smiled, smoking, saying nothing.

"Even after losing three of their own, do the McKennys number more than the Brohms?" asked Ashley.

"Yes," said Carolina. "And if you're going to ask why they don't simply overwhelm the Brohms, well, that is because of your lack of experience. Lycanthropes are fiercely protective of their own kind, even in the face of wrongdoing. They've been hunted over hundreds and hundreds of years. So, to make war, fang against claw, to kill their own kind, is rarely done."

"Except if you're the Brohms," said Ashley.

"There is also their age to consider," said Hezekiah. "All four Brohm brothers are at least one hundred years old—according to what the McKennys have written to me, anyway. They are very strong, still in the summer of their adult power. The McKennys come from an old line in Europe, but few of their elders survived the hard trip across the Atlantic, so their own pack is young, lacking leadership. And lacking in that area, they have called for advocates. Called for me, and for my sister. We have helped the McKennys before with our wealth. Now, we will help with the reputation and power the Peregrine Estate. One way or the other, the Brohms will not be allowed to so blatantly plague this immigrant people. I will not have it."

"You and Carolina run this outfit, yes?" asked

Willow, chewing over a thought in his mind. "And you have agents that are. . . specialists?"

"To put it in its simplest terms, sure," said Hezekiah, tilting his head as if wondering where Willow was going with this.

"If you have specialists for specific purposes, why did Carolina come to enlist my father's help?"

Hezekiah looked at Carolina, shaking his head. "Do these men know nothing about. . .?"

Carolina shook her head.

The big man turned back to the brothers. "Boys, I don't know how to tell you this. . . but 'round three or five years before Ashley here was born, your parents were a part of a big dust-up between a little town and a pack of these lycanthropes. A lot of people got killed."

"Dust-up? Meaning our parents were fighting werewolves?" asked Ellery.

Hezekiah smirked. "Not even remotely, cowhand. They negotiated with them. Your daddy was the biggest part of that. The lycanthropes respected his bravery and his forthrightness. Talked the whole situation off a ledge with a handshake deal with their leader. Didn't he, Mr. Stephens?"

Julius Stephens looked at the Sutliff brothers, all three, from his place across the table. "Without blinking an eye."

"Wait," said Willow. "You were there?"

"Of course," said Stephens. "I was the one who shook his hand, saving near two hundred and fifty lives."

"You're a. . ." said Ellery.

"Mr. Ellison's estate requires specialists of all sorts and kinds," said Julius, his eyes flashing like gold coins in the wavering lamplight. "And I am along on this trip to ensure that the pack line is abolished and that my people are set loose from the barony's chain."

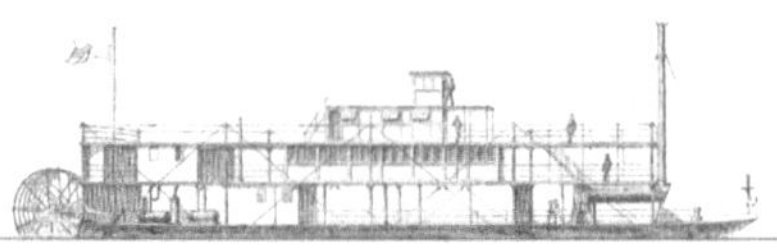

CHAPTER ELEVEN

ABOARD THE STEAMER *WHITE ROSE*, SMOKEY HILL RIVER, LITTLE KANSAS BARONY

Outside the window of Ashley's cabin, the Smoky River proved true to its name. A blanket of fog rolled over its dark, brooding waters, curling near the bank like thousands of skeletal fingers clawing for ground. He watched the fingers of fog, waiting. Until there came the knock at his cabin door. His brothers stepped into the cabin, and Ashley shut the door behind them. Ellery sat on the bed, his eyes big as dinner plates, running his fingers through his hair. He looked as young as he ever had, his mind clearly spinning at all they had discussed at dinner.

Willow went to the far side of the cabin and leaned his shoulders against the wall. He crossed his arms over his chest and looked to Ashley.

"Alright, you wanted to talk, and I'm sure I know your mind," he said, then sighed. "You have my apology for getting drunk. And for our fight".

It came so abruptly that it confused Ashley. "What? No. No, this isn't about that."

Willow bristled. "I said I apologize."

He wasn't sure why his brother was being so insistent. "Okay?"

"Your memory is for shit, brother," said Willow.

Ellery scooted forward on the bed, rubbing his hands on his pants. "If your brother apologizes. . ." he began.

Ashley remembered, and repeated words their mother had said time and time again. "Then you must accept. Yes. Yes," he said. "I accept your apology. Now, I don't like anything about all this."

"Stephens looks so normal," said Ellery, quiet awe in his voice. "Hell, not frightening at all."

"He doesn't mean that part, Ellery" said Willow. "He means the ambush."

Ashley sat down in the little chair next to the door and began to roll a cigarette. "It's not just that. Hezekiah lied to us. Brought us here on false pretenses. Which means. . . Carolina lied to us first. Lied to mother."

Willow clouded up, squeezing his arms tighter. "I don't know if I'd say—"

"You've got the eyes for Carolina," said

Ashley, plain and direct. "Put that aside. We were told that we were coming along to help in a negotiation between two parties, not to wipe out an entire group of people. Hell, we don't even know how much of what Ellison says is true."

Ellery nodded. "We don't know anything."

"Well, I trust them," said Willow. "They have no reason to lie to us."

"They have *every* reason to lie to us," said Ashley. "Every reason to play it false if it means getting it their way."

Will's anger flashed bright and hot. "This is not a goddamn game of poker, Ashley."

"*Everything* is a game of poker, brother. Everyone is pretending their cards are something less or more than they are. Pushing in wagers that work like levers against what you think to be true. Every person is a smiling liar in the table game of life. And in this game, Will, if we throw in with the wrong hand, we don't go bust. We go into the ground."

Will rolled his eyes. "Two years in St. Louis has broken your thinking."

Ashley had stomached just about enough of his simplistic, hayseed outlook. "And your goddamn summer-bird crush on this woman has—"

"Hey!" Ellery stood suddenly, putting his bulky frame between the two of them. And he certainly looked all man as he switched his gaze back and forth between the two of them. "I swear to God, if I have to hear the two of you go at each other again, I'm going get in the middle of you both and split the fuckin' difference."

"Sit down, Ellery," said Ashley. "Will here has a problem he's been trying to voice since he found me in St. Louis. Let's let him say what he needs to say, else we might lose him in a bottle again."

"Ashley, I swear to—" Ellery began, but Will put a hand on his shoulder. Ellery wrinkled his brow and sat. "Fine. If you kill each other, it'll save me the goddamn headache of hearing the two of you argue."

Ashley burrowed his eyes into Will.

His brother stared right back, just as he had done down the barrel of his gun at the Blind Crow. "Just because you were off on your own, gone from home, doesn't make you an authority on the world."

Ashley pulled on his cigarette, then blew out the smoke. "And just because you stayed home, doesn't make you the better son."

The words struck Willow, for he rocked back an inch. Ashley had ached to say them from the moment his brother had shown his face in the saloon. But Will composed himself quickly, let the comment roll by, perhaps trying to prove himself immovable by such sentiments.

"You don't trust anyone because you know

deep down you can't be trusted. And it eats at you. Gnaws on your brain." Will's eyes were wide, never before looking more like their father's. "Mother and Daddy trusted these people. That goes a long way with me."

Ashley grit his teeth, feeling the deep pain only a brother can feel when he knows a sibling is right. He took in a deep breath, let it out. "I didn't say we shouldn't go. I just said that this whole trip began under the pretense of a lie, and that, my brother, makes me un-fucking-comfortable. It makes me wary. Cautious. Consider for a moment, if you will, that when I challenged Ellison's bullshit, Stephens put his hands beneath the table. And that unnerved you, made you stop thinking about that woman and stop trusting. So much so that you felt the need to act first, because you sensed malicious intent."

Will grit his teeth. "Well, I. . . I wasn't gonna let him—let him, well, you know."

Ashley grinned, the same grin he wore just before laying down the cards of a winning hand. "I do know. And I'm only doing the same thing for us here and now. This is me bringing us together, just us, because I do not like Ellison's intent to mislead us. Because I won't let him put the two of you in danger."

"It wouldn't hurt you to trust someone, Ashley," said Willow, scraping one of his boots along the floorboard though nothing was there.

Ashley nodded, though he did not say what came into his mind. *Trusting people is the easiest way to let them hurt you, Willow.*

Later, Ashley sat in his room smoking cigarette after cigarette. He piled their stubby corpses in an ashtray near the tobacco pouch, tinder, and rolling papers. Watching the smoke fill his room and the fog rolling over the Smoky Hill, he considered the angles of what Hezekiah had said. Why he might have said it as he did. What, if any of it, was true? It had been his mother who had insisted that all three of them join their mission while Carolina had requested the help of only one. Didn't his mother's trust matter? She was smarter than most. But Ashley couldn't help but see the deception, not only in Hezekiah's treatment of the Sutliffs but also in the scheme he would enact against the Brohms.

A knock at the door startled him from his thoughts. Big and heavy, the sound made him think it was Ellery or...

"It's Hezekiah," came the deep bass voice, muffled by the wood. "Wanna talk."

"I bet you do," said Ashley to himself. Then, he got up and let the big man in. "Figured you'd come by," he said. "Have a seat."

Hezekiah took off his hat and sat in the chair where Ashley had just been sitting. He rested one hand over his knee, then set his hat atop it, his thick fingers sliding along the pinch of the crown.

Ashley sat on his bed, crossed an ankle over the other knee.

Hezekiah took a breath as if about to speak, then shook his head. His eyes moved all over the cabin.

"For a man who wants to talk, you sure don't say much," said Ashley, prodding.

Hezekiah looked down at his hat for a moment, a little smile slashing white across the black tangle of his beard. "You like to get the first blow in," he said. "In a fight, or in a conversation. I bet that's the way you play poker, too. Big bets early. Try to chase out the timid or cautious players."

Ashley nodded. "Easiest way to cash an ante pot. Do it enough times, it adds up."

"I'm sure it does." Again, he squeezed the hat's pinch, lifted it up and set it back down on his knee.

"You didn't come here to talk about poker," said Ashley.

"No. I came here to tell you that because I knew your father and your mother well, I trusted them with the truth. You, I do not know personally. All I know of Ashley Sutliff comes from your father's letters. That you are adventurous, that you love the thrill of contests, and that you locked horns with your pa because you wanted to go off to the big city. And while that may make you unique among your dutiful brothers, it makes you just like most of the men living on the Earth. You think desire for something other than what you have makes you special, when in fact, it makes you woefully common."

Ashley kept the fire of his temper low, sucked his teeth. "Well, that's quite the observation from a man who smells of bullshit every time he opens his mouth. And that, Mr. Ellison, is what makes *you* common."

"That smart tongue of yours," said Hezekiah. "For my love of your mother, I will resist the urge to yank it out of your mouth."

"Now we're talking," said Ashley, goading harder. He wanted to see where the man's pressure points were. Wanted to see the placid, stern demeanor melt away. Wanted to see every eye twitch and fake grin. Wanted to see Hezekiah Ellison's every tell and inscribe them on the wall of his memory for all time so that the man could never bullshit him again. "You're pretty big. You might be able to back that claim."

"And you're quick. You just might be able to get away."

"What makes you think I'd run?"

"Oh," said Hezekiah, long and slow. "I know a runner when I see one."

The fire inside Ashley swelled. He felt the

heat of his anger begin to boil away his charm, his control. "Is that a fact?"

"Oh yeah." Hezekiah smiled bigger than ever. "That's a fact. See, the difference between a fighter and a runner is easy to discern. Willow pulled a gun on my man in the middle of a saloon. That's a fighter. Ellery? Strong as a bull and twice as mean. Your pa said he whipped a boy five years older for bad-mouthing your mother. But you"—he lifted a hand from the hat to point at Ashley, wrist ticking back and forth like he was tapping a waning lantern—"you're a runner. You ran off from home, from responsibility. Ran to table games and drink, and whores probably. Hell, it wouldn't surprise me if you were running from a debt in St. Louis and that's why you went back home when you got word your daddy was sick. Yeah," he continued, finger pointing, "you didn't care. It just gave you another reason to run from something. Because that's what every runner longs for. What every coward looks for: a reason." The smile stretched all the way across the man's goddamn face. The tell of a man who could not hide the fact he had a winning hand.

And that was the tell that gave it away.

Hezekiah hadn't come here to argue; he'd come to see what kind of man Ashley was. To see if, in a moment of tension, he was a resource or a liability.

The realization cooled his temper. He let his eyes go heavy, relaxed, and looked away from the finger and down to the hat hiding Hezekiah's other hand. His goal was to goad Ashley into rushing him—to make him so mad that he'd charge, reach for Hezekiah—and then the hand would come up with either a little pistol or a knife, teach Ashley a lesson. Show this young Sutliff pup that he wasn't as smart or as clever as Hezekiah Ellison.

It was a subtle play for sure.

Not subtle enough.

"And what are you, Ellison?" asked Ashley, his voice cold as the river beneath them.

Hezekiah tilted his head. The smile faded and his eyes went hard. "I am an imperfect instrument trying to play a song too good for my meager sound. I am a poor brother to a marvelous woman who is ten times the person I shall ever be. I was once a part of a dreadful cult that hopes to end the world. Now, I work against them. How is that for a truth?" But he didn't give Ashley time to respond to the question. "I am a collector—not of things, but of people. People who believe in justice, even when justice requires them to sin for its sake. And I am excellent at one thing and one thing only, Mr. Sutliff: knowing exactly what I am proficient at and what I am not. While that may not get many people very far, it has certainly gotten me to where I am. It has helped me to survive, to build up my little agency, and it's put me in this room with you." Hezekiah lifted his hat, revealing an empty hand beneath.

He hadn't been holding anything. Hadn't been goading Ashley into acting. Hezekiah had just been telling Ashley the truth, giving his unvarnished opinion on his judgment of him.

"I think you're a runner, son, but you don't have to be." Hezekiah set his hat back on his head, readying to leave. "The questions you ask, the confidence you have to ask them; I think you could be something more than a gambler, though gambling is also a skill I think can be useful." He stood up, appraising Ashley. "I collect specialists of all types."

Ashley blinked, unsure. "Are you offering me a job in your agency?"

"Depends."

Ashley shrugged. "On?"

Hezekiah considered the question deeply. "If you can trust a liar who promises he'll never lie to you or your brothers ever again."

And then he bid him goodnight, leaving Ashley sitting there on the bed to chew over his misappraisal of the man's intent.

The *Rose* sounded her whistle, and outside the roustabouts called to each other. A great bell rang forth three times, and the paddle wheel began to churn the Smoky Hill once more. And the machinery of Ashley's mind rolled, steady as the paddle wheel of the steamer, brooding darkly as the black satin waters of the river.

Maybe it was the way Hezekiah had contested him, so naked and unafraid. Or was it how certain the man had been of himself? The manner in which he so brazenly admitted to faults other men would, for the sake of their shame, lie about and hide from others for the whole span of their lives.

It was this aspect of the man, Ashley knew, that had drawn his father's utter respect. The clarity of self. The glory in truth.

Hezekiah Ellison was a liar, but hell and damnation if Ashley didn't trust the man.

Morning came. The clouds bound the light, flickering bolts veined along their swollen stomachs, so dark they weaved a curtain of night for as far as there was sky. The *White Rose*, chewed up the Smoky Hill, pushing forward into the brooding twilight, carrying Willow Sutliff and his great dread for thunderstorms. Passing by his window, along the passenger deck, came Carolina Ellison, all her things bound up in her satchels and saddle bags. She wore a pretty green dress with shiny embroidery along the neck that flashed like emeralds even in the low light. She knocked at his door.

Willow opened it, holding his own bags. "Our stop?" he asked.

Carolina gave a slight smile. "The roustabouts are getting our horses from below. But before we meet the others at the landing, I wanted to say something."

Her eyes were bright, piercing. Like pearls of amber set within alabaster.

"About the other night," she said.

"I understand," said Will, apologetically. "And again, if I gave any offense, it was not my intent."

Carolina shook her head, a little ribbon of her fine brown hair fell along her cheek. "No, I—" She went to curl the strand away, but her fingers missed. She looked away for a moment, refusing to bother with the strand further. "It was. . . very flattering. You flattered me with your compliments. And I just wanted to say that while we cannot entertain that kind of relationship." She trailed off, thinking. Looking away, perhaps to another time, another place. "I wanted to say," Flustered, she looked to him again, frustrated with herself. "That it was very nice."

She swallowed hard. "You are very nice."

It was her shy, flustered demeanor set upon the beauty of her face which pushed away thoughts of the river, the dark skies and the thunderstorms living in their expanse. He felt warm, more confident than he could ever remember, as if all the clear skies he'd ever need lived within him right there. Right then.

"I think you are very nice, too, Ms. Ellison," he said.

"Please, Carolina is fine," she replied, then repeated. "Carolina is fine."

Her fingers fidgeted with her satchels, red at every knuckle. And without asking, he reached and slid his fingers over hers.

She let the handle slide from her grip, allowing Willow to take the burden from her. "You're very kind," she said.

Willow smiled, feeling light and sure. Like the gentleman his mother had raised. "It is my pleasure."

"Yes, well. . ." she said, turning. "Uhm, the others are waiting. So."

He nodded. "Happy to follow you, Carolina."

The two of them found the others waiting on the passenger deck. The steamer pushed near a wood-yard dock, where a tall man dressed fine as a dandy stood within the cut of the office door. He was smoking a clay pipe white as a finger bone, wearing a stovepipe hat, and grinning beneath a black mustache. "Hail," he called out.

The attendant near the unloading gate, a short Black freeman who was too young to be as bald as he was, called back, "Hail. Looking for pine at cottonwood prices!"

"I suggest you turn back now," the wood-yard man said, grinning, happy as you please, "as you'll not find that, or other opportunities of theft, here in the Little Kansas Barony."

"We'll, we're offloading a few," said the attendant. "Need wood, too. But don't be thinking of sharping me!"

The wood-yard man removed his hat with a flourish, bowed a little. "My friend, in the barony, fair is fair is fair."

The horses were offloaded, and when all their company began to step off the *Rose*, it was Ellery who leaned close to Willow and said, "Got you carrying her bags, I see."

Willow glowered at him. "I offered."

Ellery leaned closer, mischief in his eyes. "I. Bet. You. Did."

Willow shook his head, trying not to smile, though failing. "Come on, you big lout. Let's load up."

Hezekiah rented a wagon from the wood-yard man, cursing him to hell at the end of their negotiation. "Fair is fair is fair, my goddamn ass," he said, paying the man with a five-dollar gold piece.

They hitched Hezekiah's horse to the wagon yoke, and he took the reins. Stephens climbed up into the shotgun seat, and that's when Willow noticed that there were only five horses.

Willow saddled Martin and took him

through his paces to shake the dust out of his knees, then he rode over to where Stephens was bumping along in the moving wagon.

"What happened to your horse?" asked Willow.

Stephens stared ahead, leaning forward. Stooped like a crow. "We don't ride horses," he said. Then he turned, and those gold coins of his eyes flashed. "We eat them."

Willow leaned away, shocked.

A big smile broke across the man's face, and he laughed. "I'm just fucking with you."

Hezekiah roared with laughter, and Carolina, riding just behind him, snickered.

"You know," said Willow, half-serious and half-joking, "the more you talk, the less I like you."

"Beautiful gelding you have there. I used to have one like it myself."

"You might think you did," replied Willow quickly, "but you were mistaken. There's only one Martin. All others are pale imitations."

"Well, my pale imitation got shot out from underneath me six days ago on our way to St. Louis," said Stephens, shooting Ellison a bitter frown.

"Now that wasn't my goddamn fault," snapped Ellison "Those men were charging at *us*."

"And *why* was that, again? Please remind me

who announced, in broad daylight and with only thirty uninterrupted yards between us and them, that he was there to collect a bounty on their heads?"

Hezekiah became dismissive, lifted his eyebrows high. "That was so long ago, I can't remember. Doesn't sound like me, though."

"It sounds exactly like you," said Carolina.

There came from among the three of them a rolling laughter that revealed a previously hidden connection. More than a connection— friendship. Their laughter was the sound of living shared. Of moments he'd perhaps never know the details of, but could see in their smiles and their happy sound. The resonance of fellow-ship. The mission connecting them.

The sound made Willow feel a little sad and lonely. He had his brothers, certainly, but that was different. Brothers were supposed to laugh together; some might say they were required to do so. And it was the mixture of Julius Stephens in the siblings' gaiety that made Willow feel as though he had finally seen. . . something he didn't know he'd been missing his whole life.

And in the seeing of it, he came to want it more than anything else in the world.

The three began talking about events he had not been part of, and, although they encouraged him to stay and listen, he felt too great an outsider and a little ashamed that he had no grand stories as they did. He'd been the son of a hog farmer, turning the farm into a little ranch, yes, but not much more than that. He fell back slowly, and eventually found himself riding behind the wagon with his brothers.

The sky had cleared of clouds, and now the wild blue of the territory horizon, which ran out far as there was distance and wide as the span of time. Yellow grass sprayed up here and there, striving to find the light of the sun from beneath the January snow. The wagon chewed up a well-worn track. Surprisingly, the road was near flat as a pan..

He heard the laughter up ahead again, and imagined his father with them. "They knew him better than we ever did," he said, thinking out loud.

"Who knew what now?" asked Ashley.

"Daddy," said Willow. "Well, mother too. Those three knew our parents before we came around. I mean, can you imagine our father negotiating a peace between a pack of were-wolves and a town?"

Ashley sniffed a laugh. "I cannot imagine Daddy negotiating anything other than a hard bargain for the other party involved."

Ellery chuckled. "That's just how he was with you."

"Bullshit," said Ashley, drawing out the word

long and slow as he often did when sarcasm suited his purpose.

But Willow agreed with Ashley. Captain Forrest Sutliff was many things—he was a shrewd trader, defiant in the face of compromise—but he'd never been a negotiator. "I think maybe you got a more tempered version of Daddy than Ashley and I did," he said to Ellery.

Ashley nodded. "Damn right."

"Or," said Ellery, "maybe the two of you are just so damn hard-headed, you couldn't find the compromise within yourselves that he was willing to accept."

"Well," said Ashley. "Littlest brother may have a point, little brother."

And the smile on Ashley's face, something about it looked so familiar. A relic of Willow's childhood unearthed. He thought over all of the arguments and the strife that existed between them, past the disappointments they had leveled against one another. And he remembered that, no matter what transpired between them, they were connected in a way Julius Stephens would never know the Ellisons. And in a way, he suspected, that Carolina could never know Hezekiah.

They were the Sutliff boys. The sons of Forrest and Leigh. They shared among them a particular kind of outlook on the world given to them by their parents. And while not a one of them had lived up fully to their parents' expectations—what child could?—when they were apart, they were three independent cords cut from the same length of rope. Easily separated, but when you brought them together, they made a knot that would never lose its cinch. Never fray.

And that was the moment, all of a sudden, Willow Sutliff passed through the storm cloud of resentment that had thundered inside him since the day Ashley had left. The moment when the lightning strike question of, "How can you leave?" became the sunbeam clarity of, "I am so glad you're here."

Willow opened his mouth to say. . . something, but he could not say it here; even in this wide-open prairie, there was not enough room or privacy to unpack all that he felt for Ashley. All that he wanted to say. But he felt it all the same. And looking at Ashley looking at the horizon, Willow saw the boy who had become the man, the wasteful son he'd always call brother. No matter his flaws. No matter his choices. Ashley Sutliff was a gambler and a rake, would never settle into the homely virtues their parents touted as the height of manhood. He would be a man of the world, and though the world would certainly try to claim him, the man would always belong to Willow.

"That's Williamson," said Hezekiah called

from the front of the wagon. The Sutliffs rode to catch up and to see.

There was a dark line of shadows set along the mean between sky and land. Not too far off, a moderate creek ran east to west, its source unseen. The current ran quick, wrinkling the face of the waters, where they reflected the high, bright sun, so that the riverbank twinkled and flashed as if encrusted with gems of countless hues and sheens: a priceless sight.

"From here," Hezekiah said, "you will act with the coolest hands, boys. Be steady. Calm. Lycanthropes are quick to anger."

"How quick?" asked Ellery, joking.

"He's serious, kid," said Julius Stephens.

"As a hellfire preacher giving a sermon to the already damned," said Hezekiah. "This first day will be introductions and the fancy bullshit that these self-entitled aristocrats will want to revel in for a while. It's a little game of show and tell, with them showing us what they can give without telling me outright to rule in their favor."

"Is everyone in Williamson a lycanthrope?" asked Ashley. "I suspect not."

"Not even remotely," said Stephens. "The communities mingle our society and yours. They are a model of the difficult peace your father and I built. That model has stood for near twenty years now, though the Little Kansas Barony has made a mockery of it by starving their own kind and lording over those unlike them."

"How will we know who is human and who is not?" asked Ellery. "If I need to, that is."

"You humans can hide the predator behind your eyes," said Stephens, turning to face them from the shotgun seat. His eyes caught the sunlight, flashing gold. "My kind do not share the same adaptation."

"Follow our lead," said Carolina. "Then tonight, after we've made introductions and assessed the full situation, we'll make a plan on how to move forward."

"You mean plan on how we'll kill them," said Ellery, blunt as a nail head.

"Maybe," said Hezekiah.

"Damn it, Hezi," said Carolina. "Not may—"

"I said maybe." His words final.

"Julius," said Carolina, pleading. "Please, tell him. Again."

"Your brother has made up his mind," he said, but then turned to Hezekiah. "For your sister's sake, you should take care, friend. If you try to leverage the resolution between the Brohms and the McKennys too far in the latter's favor, there is significant risk. My people are territorial and swift to chase away threats to the dominion they see as their own."

"Hell, I know that," said Hezekiah, his temper flaring. "The more I keep chewing it over, the more I don't like it. An ambush is. . . it just feels beneath us, and beneath what I want the Peregrine Estate to become. Forrest understood that, and my God I wish he were here now to take my side. Help the rest of you see."

Those words made Willow grin with pride.

But Julius shook his head. "Captain Sutliff was a persuasive man, no doubt, but he was dealing with me, not the Brohms. An ambush is the only way you'll triumph in a fight against the four of them. Transformed, I can handle one, maybe two, if I get lucky. I am strong, friend, but no wolf is stronger than the pack."

Hezekiah said nothing, and Carolina rode in silence too.

Willow didn't care for it one bit.

"How often do your people all come together for something like this," asked Ashley. "The meeting of two packs."

"It is rare," said Julius.

"What would war mean?" asked Ashley. "How bad could it get?"

Stephens's head drooped, as if the notion took all the energy from him. "Mr. Sutliff, my people have survived this long on guile and cunning and our ability to blend in with your race. There are many, perhaps a hundred packs of varying size, within the United States alone. If these two packs were to go to war, word would spread, packs would begin to pick sides, and then. . . there would be desolation the likes of which this country has not seen since its revolution. En masse, from state to territory, you would see the bloody evidence of our conflict. All your fear would crowd over your reason, and in our vulnerable disunity you would hunt us, as you did in the lands of our mothers and fathers. For us, unlike for you, war is a never considered until there is nothing left to consider."

"That's why they can't pick another lycanthrope to help negotiate," said Willow, now understanding completely. "That's why you need an outsider."

Ashley had missed it though. "Wait, why?"

"The Brohms have to make it look like they've exhausted all possible venues, gone so far as to bring in a third-party who has no stake in either the McKennys or the Brohms."

"Which means. . ." said Carolina, as if leading Willow to the final point.

A fresh chill went through him. "They aren't coming to the negotiation in good faith. . ."

"Right," said Julius. "They don't want a truce. They want cause for war."

CHAPTER TWELVE

WILLIAMSON,
LITTLE KANSAS BARONY

Ashley followed the long, dark line of the road up the hill, trailing just behind the wagon and the other riders of their company. The winter frost ran white and clean from road to slope to the brow of the hill, all the way to Williamson. The snow powder, thrown over the face of the hill like a blanket over the sleepy world, covered all save for the single black seam of the well-traveled road, hacked up by horse and foot traffic. The sun dangled in a reaching sky the self-same color of the bluebonnets on the Sutliff acreage, which flowered every April when the little creek swelled with spring showers. Everything was white and blue, save for the burning sun and Williamson, which slowly lost its shadow, its flat black melting to textures of brown and green, its whites pale against the snow, its fading shades of blue forever the sky's inferior.

At the top of the hill, the commercial section of the city ran as one long street, and just beyond were squat row homes, and beyond them were homesteads, little more than vague impressions on the prairie except for the columns of smoke rising from their chimneys.

The company rode along the main thoroughfare, quickly becoming the subject of every gaze. Ladies carrying parcels wrapped in butcher paper looked at them from beneath white bonnets. Striding cattle hands crossed their path, never slowing but giving them keen glances just beneath the brim of hats slanted across their faces. Carpenters ceased their sawing on lumber meant for a constellation of unmoving builders framed in the cross-beams an unfinished steepled building too narrow to be a bank, too long to be a schoolhouse.

"Guessing they don't get a lot of company," said Ellery. He smiled and tipped his hat to a woman passing by. "Not terribly friendly."

"They are a whole town sharing a secret," replied Hezekiah. "You'd be wary, too."

From a long way off, a short man in a black suit came out of what looked like a town hall of some type and hurried toward them. He was portly and ran as though the act viciously disagreed with him. One hand pumped from side to side, the other kept a bowler hat pinned atop his head. "Mr. Ellison?" he hollered from near thirty yards away. "Mr. Ellison?"

Hezekiah slowed the wagon and raised a hand to signal the others to do the same. He waited. Ashley saw a smile on his face, as if he were enjoying the man's humorous dash.

"Mr. Ellison, sir!" The man was near breathless, flushed red by the time he reached the wagon. "I. . ." he wheezed. "Mister Elli— Whew, my emphysema does not. . ." He went to hacking and coughing and wheezing. "You will pardon my. . ." Again the coughing took over. Finally, swallowing hard and struggling to catch his breath, he said, "Mr. Ellison and company, yes?"

"Take your time. I'd hate for you to keel over in the street," said Hezekiah. "And yes, you name me true."

The man smiled, placed a hand on his chest as if apologizing for some great inconvenience. "My name is Quietly. Jake Quietly. I'm the—"

"The Brohms' man, yes. My god, Mr. Quietly, catch your breath."

He shook his head, smiling. "I am afraid it is always running from me. Listen, you've arrived just in time. The McKennys' representatives are meeting with the Brohm brothers now. I would be glad to escort you and your people inside and announce your arrival."

"They began talks without me?" asked Hezekiah, his voice lowered. Beveled to carry an edge.

"The McKennys were incensed. You must understand that since our last correspondence the tension has. . . risen near to a fever pitch, I am afraid. Stellan Brohm challenged Issac McKenny to a duel just last night and, my employers are leaning into the conflict against my stringent advice." Quietly gulped air, going nearly blue in the face. "The duel is scheduled for today, and right now the leadership of both families are in the Hall. Which is why I ran, hoping all the way that it was you and your—"

"Move," said Hezekiah, giving Quietly only half a second to comply. He whipped the reins and drove the wagon quickly toward the conflict inside the Town Hall. Mud spattered the air, just missing Ashley, who followed along with his brothers.

The town hall, two-and-a-half stories and painted green as a pine tree from threshold to slatted roof, was trimmed with brass lattice windows and looked just about as grand a building as one might find in this part of the world. The door, simple save for a heavy brass knocker the size of a bullring, still hung ajar after Quietly's exit. Hezekiah hopped down from the wagon with a grace that surprised Ashley. A man that size, moving that nimbly, now that was something to behold. The others dismounted and followed Hezekiah's lead, into the sunlit grand hall where the sound of the inner chaos of debate boomed near out into the street.

Standing the doorway, just before he entered in, Hezekiah turned to face the five following him. "Do nothing," he said, that sharp-enough-to-shave edge in his words. "Say nothing. Watch me. Act if I do."

"Of course," said Carolina, insulted that the man had suggested the notion.

"I am talking to the Sutliffs," he said, and it was Willow and Ashley who got the baleful eye of his countenance. "And I mean it, boys. Our actions in this time and place could mean hundreds of lives, human and lycanthrope alike. You are here in case it comes to violence and if it does, you must act quickly."

"We hear you," said Ashley. "It's tense."

"No," snapped Hezekiah. "It's a gunpowder cache."

"Like he said," piped Willow. "We hear you."

And then Hezekiah Ellison's face, flushed and wrinkled with insistence, suddenly smoothed. He smiled big and bright, entirely disarming, removing the mask of command to reveal the disposition of a carnival crier. He turned and walked down the short hallway and turned left to face a massive cased opening unto the town hall floor. The blast of arguments and angry voices and the bellowing of furious men filled the hall, assaulting every wall.

"Gentleman," said Hezekiah, illuminated by a beam of afternoon sun as if stepping out behind the curtain of the frontier, onto the Little Kansas Barony Stage. They the audience. He the heralding Chorus that would set into motion the play they would share.

The arguments still boomed, as if none in the unseen room had heard his voice.

Ashley watched from down the hall. "They aren't going to listen."

Carolina looked back at him, smirking. "No?" she asked. "Watch."

"A pack of wolves," cried Hezekiah, who then brought his hands together so sharply it made a tremendous thunderclap of noise.

And the unseen lamenters within the town hall settled, the wave of their voices crashing upon his words, hushing to a foamy silence.

"A pack of wolves, I find," Hezekiah said, still standing in the bar of light. "Lost amid discord so great that they look to the sky and call forth their friend, the falcon. And he hopes they will see, beyond and higher than the silhouette of his outstretched wings, the moon their mother, and remember that for all their discord, every pack is the wolf and every wolf the pack."

There was the shuffling of feet. Then, a single, low chuckle.

Hezekiah lifted a finger, and silence returned. "For those of you who do not know the scent of my person or the shape of my face, I am Hezekiah Ellison." Then, looking to his sister, smiled at her. He gestured for her to join him. "This is my dear sister, Carolina Ellison, half-owner and the whole brains of the Peregrine Estate."

Carolina stepped into the bar of light, wrapped an arm around her brother's waist, and waved to the people Ashley could not see.

"My sister and I bring with us four body men: one of your kin and three of our own. These are Mr. Julius Stephens, by way of the hunting grounds of French Canada; and the three brothers Sutliff, by way of their late father Forrest and widowed mother Leigh, whose reputations and honor you will find equally measured in the boys they raised. You will meet them in time," said Hezekiah pausing. Then, leaning a sterner look unto the crowd, the man stiffened. "I have been called to this place by Albert Brohm and Fionn McKenny to fulfill a solemn duty. I was informed that there would be no meetings among the packs until I arrived, so you can understand my concern in discovering that before I even arrived to fulfill my promise, you have already broken yours."

He paused. The room so quiet before him.

"What am I to think?" he asked, so confident.

Every word searing. "Friends, tell me if I have wasted my time in hasted travel only to find the gulf too wide for us to build a bridge of compromise. If so, my company and I will be on our way, soured and never to prospect a favor for your kind ever again. Because if you cannot be trusted with your word, you cannot be trusted at all. Wolf or pack."

From the unseen room came a deep voice, saying only, "Bold."

"Never let it be said that I was timid," said Hezekiah.

"The scent of you proves true as the reputation preceding it," said the voice, deep and refined, fiercely aristocratic. "Please, bring your people in."

The brothers Sutliff, all three, followed Julius and the Ellisons into the grand hall. What the near three stories of grandeur outside only suggested, the interior of the building announced outright. From the polished hickory speaking floor and encircled seating of the finest carpentry to the topmost skylight cut from stained glass, the room shone as though it had never seen use. At the center, a silver-haired man with a jaw stiff as an anvil stood, broad-shouldered and dressed finer than any dandy Ashley had ever seen. He stood upon a raised dais, where the beams lancing from the skylight colored him in glory.

When Ashley looked upon the man on the dais, the people surrounding him became only vague impressions, for Ashley was so drawn to him. Drawn to his eyes. To his undeniable strength. The power radiating off him was brighter than the light that robed him.

"I am Albert Brohm, second of my litter," he said. "If it were to be said there was a first among the Brohm pack, the pack would assert that I am he."

"And who speaks for the other party," asked Hezekiah, seemingly resistant or perhaps outright immune to the irrepressible magnetism that had so quickly taken Ashley. "Where is Fionn McKenny?"

"I am here," came a voice from the back of the hall. A figure stood up and strode out of the balcony's shadow, tall and long, and dignified despite the brown threadbare clothes he wore. "It is good to put a face to the man we owe so much." Fionn's voice simmered with strength, but not, Ashley thought, to the same degree as Albert Brohm's. "I am glad you have arrived to serve the Doom Seat for our strife."

Doom Seat? Ashley didn't know what the hell that meant, and he certainly didn't like the sound of it.

"Then give me the simple right of it all," said Hezekiah. "Testify your grievances. I will hear them now."

"Yes," agreed Albert Brohm. "Above all else, your impartial judgment will help us avoid any more needless bloodshed."

"We've shed no blood on our side, Silver-Mane," said Fionn. "It's you and your brothers and your militia driving our pack from the hunting ground. Men who take Brohm money with one hand and strike us with the other. We will suffer this indignity no more."

At that, near a dozen men and women on one side of the room burst with a cheer.

Brohm said nothing, letting the outburst fade, and then brought his hands from behind his back and raised his palms. "You were expelled from a land that no longer feared your strength and crossed an ocean of troubles on the coin of a human patron. You were allowed into Little Kansas, provided trails and tracks of land suitable for your needs. Yet your kin hunted outside the plenty that was given. Is it not our way to punish those who stalk into the lands of another pack?"

"Plenty," Fionn said, incensed. "Plenty? You've choked the pack line. Partitioned hunting grounds to such a degree that—"

"I will not be put at a disadvantage by the tempers that flared before I arrived." Hezikiah boomed as he strode to the dais. He turned to the light-glorified Albert Brohm. "Am I to sit the Doom Seat?"

Brohm looked back to the McKennys. "Have we an official accord on our Judge?"

"Yes," said Fionn without hesitation.

Brohm nodded. "I relinquish the seat and name you Judge Ellison, for so long as you will wear the mantle."

Hezekiah stepped atop the platform.

For the rest of his days, Ashley Sutliff would remember, with such clarity, the precise moment that Hezekiah Ellison took that stage and placed the neck of the Little Kansas Barony between his teeth.

They watched the Judge patiently and intently lean his ear to their troubles and conflicts, their new hatreds and their old ways. He took control with charm and swift tongue, charted his way across old slights, and navigated the unknown ones brought to his attention. Sitting next to Carolina, Ashley marveled, and the woman beside him grinned that knowing grin of hers the whole time.

When the day's arguments were winding down, Willow heard Carolina softly say to Ashley, "And you said they wouldn't listen," she said, sniffing a laugh. "When my brother enters a room, he is seen. When he speaks, he is heard. And when he listens"— she blew out a little breath across her lips, not quite a whistle—"the speaker feels like the only person alive."

"Today's hearing is concluded," said Judge Ellison, one hand lifted as though he were taking an oath. "We will resume tomorrow, 10 a.m. sharp. As a measure of early compromise and good will, I propose that tonight, all Brohm hunting grounds shall be made available to the empty stomachs of each McKenny. Every McKenny will eat their fill and promises to take no more than their hunger requires, storing nothing for later days. What say you?"

Albert Brohm made a graceful gesture, as if this compromise meant little to him or, perhaps nothing at all.

Fionn McKenny looked to his pack, each of them hot-eyed at the prospect, lips wet with anticipation.

Willow saw the wolf in their eyes, the golden moon living behind their counterfeit colors of brown and green, hazel and blue. The thrill of the hunt. The want for blood. And that sight awoke an ancient fear inside him, something primal. Something that made him want to have his hands close to a weapon and his feet near a fire.

"So mote it be then," said Judge Ellison.

"Happy hunting," said Albert Brohm to the McKenny pack. "May your prey slip and falter."

And with those words, the two dozen

McKennys did not carefully usher themselves out of the town hall, but ran from the building and out into the street, where there came a great noise: cries of feral jubilation that rounded their shape into wild howls so deep and loud and terrible that they chilled the blood running in Willow's veins.

Albert Brohm, now partitioned by three other men dressed in frock coats of sable gray and black, strode over to where Willow and the others were rising to their feet.

The four lycanthropes were kin, that was easy to tell by the way they walked, the shared silver running through their thick, well-coifed hair, and the pride in their stern, smooth-shaven faces.

"It would be rude of me to say what I am thinking," Albert Brohm said to Carolina, "certainly before I have had a chance to introduce myself and my kin to you, Ms. Ellison. My worldly manners have saved me from my desire to be bold. I am Albert Brohm, these are my brothers Stellan, Michael, and Charles." From left to right, each gave a polite nod at being named. They were all handsome, tall, and sheened in confidence.

Willow did not like the hungry, charming smiles on their faces or the gold flashing behind their eyes.

"It is my pleasure to meet the four of you,"

said Carolina, giving a little bend at the knee that Willow hated more than the hunger in the Brohm's faces. "And it is to my delight that your manners have overruled your boldness, Mr. Brohm."

"It is Mr. Brohm to the rest of your company," said Albert, "but not to you, Ms. Ellison. Honor me. Call me by my name."

Willow didn't know if the Carolina's coy smile was genuine, but it made him feel a certain way. A way that over the course of his life had made him prone to anxiety, but in this moment made him act.

"My name is Willow Sutliff, Mr. Brohm," he said, stepping toward the lycanthrope. "This is our eldest Ashley, and our little brother Ellery. We are the sons of Captain Forrest Sutliff, who is known to you for the peace he negotiated with Mr. Stephens here. It is my pleasure to make your acquaintance." He extended a hand.

Albert Brohm slanted his eyes down to the waiting palm, then back up to Willow's gaze. "Ah," he said, "the human custom of shaking hands. It has never agreed with me or my brothers. You will forgive me if in my own house I keep my own ways."

"He is still green in the way of customs," said Hezekiah, joining them. "But a greater complement of able fellows you will not find among our number, all three of them without peer."

"I'm certain," said Brohm. "In honor of your visit, we have had a meal prepared for you. My brothers and I will refuse the hunt tonight, as in solidarity of your coming, we wish to share your table manner. Everyone is invited, of course, but I would be remis if I didn't request for you"—he turned his gaze back to Carolina—"to sit at my right hand."

Carolina blushed a deeper shade of red. "I would be happy at that," she said.

Willow's insides twisted and his jaws turned to millstones.

"Alright," said Hezekiah, stepping between wolf and prey. "Lay down the weapons of charm. I'm hungry, and we have much to discuss."

They walked single file toward a door opposite the entry, and the whole way Willow wished he'd been the one to interject. He didn't totally know why. Carolina had simply been nice to him, roused him in close but mostly polite conversation. Hadn't expressed anything other than gratitude for his kindness. Hell, she'd quickly rejected his single, straight-forward advance only two nights prior. Still, he felt what he felt: an overwhelming requirement to ensure her protection.

Just out a southern doorway, they came to a covered pavilion where a circle of tripod fires whipped their curling light across lengths of dining tables.

"I hope you will find our table settings to your liking," said Albert Brohm, leading the way. "Our cook has prepared fried chicken, snapped peas, collard greens, and a dessert I cannot even pronounce."

"*Gâteau de mille-feuilles*," said Stellan Brohm, his words smooth, quick, like a sharp blade slides across glass.

"That's the one." Albert stopped at the table closest to them and gestured at the seats. The tables were apportioned six chairs to each, fine and polished, sashed in white silk runners. Tall glasses stood glimmering next to silver platters and matching dinnerware. "Stellan will sit with the Sutliff brothers here. I am sorry to split your party, but you understand. Yes?"

"It's no problem at all," said Hezekiah, eyeing the Sutliff brothers and compelling them to accept without retort.

Willow didn't like the idea of being out of earshot from the other table, but he didn't argue. He would follow Hezekiah's lead. Do as the man required.

"Why, I think it would be fine if we pulled these tables together," said Carolina, not asking. She placed a delicate hand on Albert Brohm's chest. "Mr. Brohm. . . Albert, if you would so kindly humor me. You see, I have spent so little time with the Sutliff boys, and it would be my delight if they would remain nearby." She threw a playful smirk at Hezekiah. "My brother is quick to compromise. And that is good, for that is his purpose here." Her hand slowly slid from Brohm's chest until it ended as an index finger, pointed at where the man's heart should be. "I am more direct. A simple woman, easily satisfied with having my way. You will do this for me, yes?"

Ashley leaned close to Willow. "Close your mouth, little brother," he said in a low voice so only the two of them could hear. "Flies might nest inside."

Willow snapped his jaws closed. Carolina had become so. . . different from who she truly was. It was the way her eyes had gone smoky, her lips pursed fully with every word. He side-eyed Ashley. Of course, his older brother was grinning.

"I gather from your words that you are not one to be put off or refused anything, Ms. Ellison," said Albert Brohm. With a snap of his fingers and a twirl of his wrist, he ordered the attendants to do as Carolina had asked.

As the tables were being repositioned, Carolina moved away from Brohm to stand next to Willow, so close he could smell the scent of her flowery perfume. And under the sound of the tables and chairs being moved, she leaned close and whispered, "Sit next to me."

Willow said nothing, only nodded, his heart pounding.

Albert sat at the head of the table. To his left sat his brothers, then Julius next to Ellery. Opposite Albert, at the foot seat, sat Hezekiah Ellison. To his left, back up toward the host sat Ashley, then Willow next to Carolina at Albert's right hand.

Albert lifted his hand, snapped twice. Attendants in fine brown suits, right arms curtained with crimson serving cloths, began to serve the dinner from deep sterling pots with practiced skill. They were all human, Willow guessed, for the lack of gold in their eyes. The plates were filled to the edge with hot fried chicken and steaming sides. Wine, red as the blood from an open wound, filled their glasses.

The conversation was light at first as everyone ate politely, save for Ellery who stuffed his face like a squirrel storing nuts for a long winter. No one seemed to mind the youth though, as the Ellisons and Albert Brohm owned the conversation. Willow listened to Albert flatter Carolina and then ask her about her journey to the Little Kansas Barony.

The chicken was delicious, but Willow found that he had little appetite, so he mostly picked at the food politely and pretended that he was full. He drank none of the wine, remembering the promise he had made to himself on the *White Rose.*

"So it seems," said Albert, "river travel agrees with you."

"It does," she said. "But I much prefer a horse. Wind in my hair. Racing a friend." And, surprising him, she looked to Willow.

He gave a smile, unsure of what to say.

"Ah," said Albert. "I take it Mr. Sutliff here is such a friend. An accomplished rider, are you?"

"My horse, Martin, does the work. I mostly stay out of the way."

"I've always loved horses." The lycanthrope's hands were cupped palm-over-fist, and he stared intently at Willow, an intensity hidden behind his politeness. "They run so fast and for so long, but"—he paused, one eye widening greater than the other—"I've never had one outrun me. I wonder if your Martin could prove the exception to my century of experience."

"Take care, kin," said Julius Stephens from down the length of the table. "The boy knows a threat when he hears one. And so do I."

Knives ceased to slice. Wine glasses ceased to rise to lips. And an airless silence filled that open space, save only for the hushed roar of the tripod fires.

"Julius," said Hezekiah, "we don't want to insult our host."

"No," said Albert, eager to hear. "I am not

insulted, only intrigued. Kin Julius, do you hear a threat in my words?"

Julius brought his tall shoulders high, took a deep breath. "That was rude of me," he said. "Judge Ellison speaks true. You are my blood-kin. This is your table and not my place to correct you while we eat in the human manner."

Albert shrugged, breathing out a silent laugh. "And if we were not dining in the human fashion?"

"There's no need to suffer a hypothetical." Julius glared at Brohm, the predator behind his eyes peeking out. Eyes flashing gold.

"Julius—"

"No, Judge," said Albert, keeping his attention locked on Julius. "As you said, my kin, it is my table. I am host, and in the human fashion, I would have your answer. You disapprove of my words?"

"I disapprove of you," said Julius. "Your words. Your treatment of the McKenney pack. Your abuse of the pack-line. The way you've turned humans into your servants, cut off trade along the Smoky Hill to further secure your dominion. But, as you have reminded all so many times, these are your hunting grounds. You have marked them clearly."

Stellan, Michael, and Charles had all become very still. They stared at Julius and what Willow saw in those gazes sent gooseflesh down his arms, every hair going turgid along the back of his neck. And though it was chill, his hands begin to sweat.

Albert Brohm, still lacquered in unassailable calm, wiped the corners of his mouth. "You disapprove of the peace I maintain between our kind and the humans—"

"Do not speak of the peace brokered between them and us," said Julius, the gold in his eyes flashing hot and wild. "I was there when it was made."

"You are as bold as your reputation suggests, Kin Julius."

"Your reputation proves true, too, Kin Albert. What you have isn't peace; it's the threat of desolation."

"I think it is best if we retire," said Hezekiah. "I wouldn't want our—"

"I am their desolation," said Albert, so calm, so clear. The words an irrepressible truth from his mouth. "It is good that they know it, kin. And it is well that you, along with the McKennys and all other packs, know that so far as the scent of me reaches, to each corner of my territory, my ways are higher than their ways."

"Your ways," said Julius, a cuss in its sound. "That disregards the way of the pack. Your man Mr. Quietly told us that Stellan challenged Issac McKenny to a duel. You know that would rend a conflict open among our kind."

"Did I not bring together the packs?" asked Albert. "Into the Town Hall I brought them all, that the duel might be avoided. Did I not call this *man* here"—he jutted a finger at Hezekiah—"to mediate compromise to our pestilential conflict."

"A conflict you constructed by making your-selves little kings on a small hill. Stifling their hunting, Albert? Seriously, do you think none of the other packs will see clearly what you are doing here?"

"Gentleman," said Carolina. "Please—"

"Quiet, cow," snapped Albert Brohm, his voice coming from a low, primeval place. "Kin Julius, you wet your lips with accusations. You insult me at my own table. You dishonor me in both their fashion and ours. And here you are, bold Julius Stephens, peacemaker among their kind and exile among ours, challenging a pack of four when you are but one."

Julius stood, brought himself to his full height. "These are your hunting grounds, Brohm, and I adhere to the old customs. We do not challenge that which has already been marked. You asked if I disapprove. Now you have my answer, and the answer of other elders whose long ear has caught the sound of the choices you've made. You've made the right man the Judge of the Doom Seat, and if you hear chal-lenge in my voice, you mishear my call. You hear my anger and my sadness, kin, at seeing how you built a barony for yourself at the cost of a shared nation."

The Brohm brothers stared at Julius Stephens with malice in their eyes.

"This meal is over," said Albert, seething. "I have *apportioned* rooms for each of you at our hotel. I will settle my dispute with the McKennys, and I expect the full measure of Judge Ellison's honesty when he reports on the so-called *long ear* of the other packs."

Hezekiah rose, nodding at his company to follow his lead. "And you will have it. Tomorrow, I will pass a judgment that will see an end to this conflict."

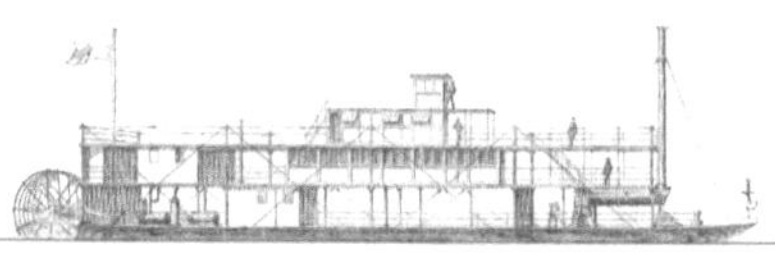

CHAPTER THIRTEEN

THE HARVEST MOON HOTEL
WILLIAMSON,
LITTLE KANSAS BARONY

"Well, you sure as fuck didn't follow my goddamn lead," said Hezekiah Ellison, pacing the large upstairs room at the Harvest Moon Hotel. "You could have warned me, Julius."

The way he puffed his pipe, plodding from one window to another, reminded Ashley of a smoking train making a little circuit.

"Warned you?" said Julius. "When a wolf howls, his kin answer back. He asked, I answered."

Hezekiah stopped his pacing, stabbed a finger at him. "You put it all at risk for that? And here you are, without a single stain of remorse or apology for it."

"I do not apologize for how I interact with my own kin. And before you fucking-well ask, Hezekiah, I do not require you to understand why. Nothing is ruined, nothing is at risk."

And that was the phrase Ashley had been afraid to hear. "I'm not getting in the middle of you two," he said, "but Hezekiah has a point. You shoved all-in before the final cards were dealt."

Julius rubbed the bridge of his nose. "If I have to hear another fucking poker metaphor..."

"How's this," said Ashley, not caring for his tone. "You fucked our advantage. Spooked the goddamn prey. How does that one fit, wolfman?"

Julius snapped his gaze to Ashley, the irises flaring like smelting gold. "You forget yourself."

"See?" asked Ashley. "Look how fucking easy it is to draw the rage out of you. Which is exactly what Brohm did to you at the table, only you're either to dumb or too prideful to see it. The long ear of the other packs? You threatened him. And how will he react? Whatever he was planning, thought he had more time to enact, you can guarantee he will accelerate it. You had him in a corner he didn't know he was in—dead to rights if we wanted to spring the ambush tomorrow in the Town Hall. No chance at that now."

"Ashley," said Carolina. "He made a mistake. Let's not relive it." She was sitting on the queen bed, staring at the floor, despondent.

"The Town Hall is no longer safe ground," said Willow. "We know the mediation is a farce, and it's likely the Brohms know we know."

"Which means?" asked Ellery, shoulders resting against an oak wardrobe just barely taller than he.

"If I judge in favor of the McKennys tomorrow, the Brohms would likely lose their claim to the pack line, which Albert cannot allow," said Hezekiah, standing before a window and gazing out onto the moonlit thoroughfare below. "The McKennys, if given full range of hunting ground, would in time grow strong enough to take by sheer numbers what the Brohms now hold with influence."

"You said that goes against the old laws," Ashley said to Julius. "That you don't challenge hunting grounds."

"A wolf doesn't challenge the pack, but packs may mark a claim if they believe they're better suited to control the pack line. In the old countries, pack-lines had been established for generations, making a challenge unlikely. But here in America, they are newer, challenged more frequently."

"Which is why Brohm prefers a pack war," said Carolina.

"Exactly," said Julius. "The old laws required him to take the McKennys in. But he can only starve them for so long. Right now, they are weak, and I have no doubt that if the four Brohm brothers attacked, they would rend their way through the McKennys without suffering too great a loss. When I saw the McKennys, got the scent of them, I knew that they are near broken. If the duel had been allowed to happen, it would have sparked a conflict, and we'd have ourselves the start of a war not seen since before my time."

Carolina sighed. "What do we do, Hezi?"

"The McKennys will be stronger tomorrow," he said, "after feeding tonigh—"

"Get back!" Julius cried.

There was a moment in his life when Ashley Sutliff was sure of how the natural world operated—could understand the rise and fall of the sun, the growing of things, breath, movement, and the want for survival that fear transforms to action—but when he saw Julius Stephens stretch and stretch, expand and further expand, his skin splitting along the slant of his gaunt face, Ashley realized he knew nothing. He watched how Julius's flesh tore away with the growth of black fur, how his fingers elongated into beveled claws and his teeth slashed to ivory daggers. How the gold in the eyes shoved past the counterfeit human color.

How all of the things that had been Julius Stephens sloughed away within the span of two heartbeats, so that he became a. . .

There would never be a word for it.

One moment Julius was one thing, and then all at once he was something greater. And that thing was so terrible, so undeniably superior to every other creature living upon the Earth, that Ashley threw his face into his hands, wholly unmanned, and began to scream.

And in the darkness of his palms, he heard a cataclysm of sounds: wood splintering, people yelling, snarling and snapping and heated inhalations, all culminating in a firmament-shattering howl. Illimitable. Roiling with power. Singular.

And then another howl answered the first, just as primal. Its sound made a crater within his memory.

Tremendous bodies moved within the room that was now much too small for the impossible creatures set within its walls. And there came such wailing and terror and screaming. Sounds assaulted Ashley's ears. Hezekiah shouting commands. Carolina saying something that sounded like a plea. He thought he heard Ellery shriek. And Ashley felt such a coward, to be so quickly made craven by the sound and the sight. The embarrassment of his shame sparked the pride within and the fires of rage ignited his heart, hot as a comet blazing across the sky. He slid his hands away from his face, remembering every single word Carolina had said about a transformed lycanthrope, but he reached for his revolver and for violence as fast as a man might do anything.

Two great beasts struggled in the center of the room, locked on each other with claws laced. They each braced against the other's power, the curved sheen of their long teeth revealed. Julius snarled, bristling with black fur, and the other—ruddy masked and hot-eyed—snapped with a slavering mouth stretched wide as the jaw's hinge would allow. With a lance of its neck, it bit hard into Julius's shoulder, spun quickly on its heel, and threw him across the room. His massive form collided with Hezekiah and smashed through the window, taking the large man with him into the moonlit night.

Pistol in hand, seeing nothing but the bestial target, Ashley cocked the hammer.

"No, Ashley," screamed Carolina. "Run!"

He fired.

The bullet struck the lycanthrope's skull, and the beast winced as if wasp-stung and snapped its ferocious gaze toward Ashley.

Looking into those cavernous sockets, burning at the center with the golden fire of predatorial dominance, Ashley Sutliff looked death square in the eye. Regret and pride, fortunes gained and squandered life mingled within Ashley as the werewolf lifted itself erect and raised a razor-clawed hand.

A shot rang out.

The lycanthrope, stung again, turned back, growling.

In the space opened by the predator's pivot, Ashley saw Willow with revolver in hand, cold-eyed and mean and unshaken by the thing before him. Smooth and viper-quick, his palm snapped down on the hammer three times. The gun roared—that gunpowder sound made by men that over generations the wolf had come to fear—and one, two, three, the shots struck the lycanthrope, the first two sinking deep into its shoulder, the third blowing half an ear away, misting the flesh to blood.

Another shot pealed, this from the other side of the room, where Ellery was pointing and firing and screaming wildly. "Die, you fuck. Die! Die! Die!"

The lycanthrope curled into itself, huddling as its massive bulk folded, arms crossing across the enormous head. With every shot the thing appeared to diminish in its purpose and aspect, blood arced from wounds greater than a dozen fold spattering across the floor and walls, spraying the hands and clothes and faces of the pistoleers.

Ashley, buffeted by the courage of his brothers, joined them in the assault. And there, in that upper room, the unrelenting gunfire volley came from the Sutliff brothers, all three. All them accurate as their father had made them, mean as their mother had ever allowed them to be.

Their fingers drew back hammers, pulled impotent triggers in polished reflex, until the room was filled with only clouds of gun smoke and the sound of clicking cylinders.

They reached for their gunbelts without word, snagging bullets to reload.

"Is it—" Ellery began and never finished as a long arm lanced out from the pillar of smoke. The back of the lycanthrope's hand caught him across the face with such force that he flew back, colliding with the oak wardrobe, causing it to collapse around him.

Then there came a growl from within the pillar of smoke, and the massive lycanthrope rose tall and strong, undiminished by the wounds the brothers had inflicted.

"Boys, run!" cried Carolina, and they proved her last.

With a single downward stroke of its claws, Carolina Ellison was shredded from scalp to throat to torso.

Willow screamed.

Ashley saw it. Saw it all so well through the smoke that he fumbled and dropped his gun, so terrible was the sight of the woman's open throat shorn to the spine, and of the blood and muscle and fat exposed, that it seemed a violation of the world. She opened her mouth as if to breathe deep, then swayed as she clutched the gaping wound and fell to the floor.

Ashley had to get to his gun, and this thought which saved his life, for when he bent to reach for the revolver, a swift wind cut the air above his head. And he howled to Willow, "Get Ellery! Get out of here!"

Moonlight pierced the shattered section of the wall, pouring in as one great shaft to illuminate not the eyes of the lycanthrope, but the eyes of the man who faced him.

Willow, tall and proud, filled with wrath, did not run for escape or for the rescue of his brother, but charged the lycanthrope. Pistol in hand, bathed in the blue incandescence of the January moon, Willow Sutliff rolled beneath a swiping paw. And it was so easy to see what he was doing, to discern the simpleness of his destructive intent. With the surest eye that Ashley would ever see, Willow pressed the four inch barrel of the revolver into the breast of the beast, and firing, attempted to reach the centuries old life of the wolf. Over and over and over he fired.

The lycanthrope took Willow in its grip, letting the bullets pass through its flesh, ribbons of blood spraying into the open air. And with a single, separating tug, as one might rend a cotton sheet, he split Willow Sutliff from neck to breastbone.

A noise came from Ashley, the sound of inhuman shock. The shattering of the heart, signaling the half-death of a man who must, after this moment, go on living.

And he wanted to act, to have his revenge, wanted to kill and destroy. But his destruction in the face of Willow's annihilation was too great. And in his great failing to protect that which mattered most, he failed to act at all.

"No," the word so soft from his lips, his greatest disbelief.

The lycanthrope, breath steaming and muscles rippling, lifted its mouth to the sky and announced utter triumph. The primordial sound of the world's greatest hunter lording over its greatest prey. Before Ashley's eyes, the sphincter-like exit wounds in its bloody fur were already healing, squeezing closed. Trimmed in silver moonlight and as terrible as beauty can make a destroyer, the lycanthrope snapped its eyes onto him. It lifted huge claws still slick with Willow's blood, and advanced.

And it was in that moment that Ashley Sutliff, frozen in the coldest terror he would ever know, saw beyond the predator. His concept of reality shattered in such a way that he looked beyond his oncoming death to see the child living within him, standing in the tall grass field of his mind. The boy who had run into thunderstorms, run away from home to St. Louis, run from the hog farm. From his mother and father. From his brothers. From all responsibility and first-born requirement. He saw the boy who looked weak and afraid, powerless to do anything but to run into the high growth all over again. Run and run and run.

"No," he said again, louder now. Angry.

The lycanthrope stepped forward, its footfalls shaking the floor and the furniture upon it.

Ashley looked down slowly and, taking his eyes from the monster, gazed at the revolver he knew could never kill such a thing. Resigned himself to die if it meant never running again.

The walls shook again beneath the unhurried stalking of the beast.

Ashley loaded the pistol, lifted it so that he stared down the iron sight. And he threw his scrutiny into the hot, glowing eyes so filled with hunger and malice. "Come on," he said, cold and sharp, unmolested by fear. "I will not suffer to wait."

The beast gave a growl, leaned back ready to pounce.

Ashley fired. The shot was true, skinning a long, hot line across the thing's scalp. And as its chin lifted from the impact, there came a roar with the gun's repeat.

Through the shattered window, where the

moon slanted into the haze of the room, Julius Stephens clawed his way back into the room, snarling. He barreled across the room without hesitation, black fur sheened in moonlight, and ducked low then came up, jaws wide. He bit down upon the lycanthrope's throat, turned, and with all his tremendous power, began to shake the Brohm brother. There was an inhuman yip and squeal and then, with the final, hard shake, something like the sound of a great tree limb breaking.

The lycanthrope in his jaws went slack. Julius shook the body again and again, his teeth sinking so deep into the tissue that blood foamed about his muzzle. Then, he set his claws upon the shoulders and wrenched, tearing the head from the lycanthrope's body. Blood fountained from the neck, spraying him in the glory of his kill. His chest rose, and his exhalation spattered the room with blood and filled it with the steam of his breath.

His golden eyes went wide, and he lifted his wet face to the sky and savagely howled.

And quickly as he had shown his true self, Julius Stephens diminished, shrinking back into the human artifice. Naked skin cool and white against the moonlight, he swiveled his head back and forth to assess the room.

Then, through the shattered doorway across the room, came Hezekiah Ellison. He rushed in, panicked and gray faced, clutching his left arm close to his chest. "Where is—"

But Ashley was running across the room to where Willow lay. He fell to his knees at the sight before him. Willow Sutliff, split at the center, the whole of him clothed in blood. And, to Ashley's great horror, his brother's eyes were moving—so wide and terrified, unable to comprehend. His mouth moved as though he were trying to speak, but no words came forth.

"Willow," he said, sliding his brother's broken body upon his knees. "Willow?"

Willow opened his mouth again, and he inhaled. Ashley felt his brother's body rise, crest like a wave, then sag. His brown eyes, as bright and beautiful as they had ever been, searched Ashley's, asking a question he could not say.

From across the room, so far, far away, Hezekiah wept openly. "Carolina. Carolina. Carolina," he pleaded.

"Please, little brother," cried Ashley. Tears quickly forming in his tired eyes, fell from eye to cheek to chin to land upon his brother's brow. "I *am sorry* that I left," he said, the words collapsing beneath the weight of sorrow. "I am so sorry I was gone."

Willow shuddered, blinked hard and long in reply.

"Hold on to me," said Ashley.

And Willow, with fading strength and

childish desperation, wrapped his arms around his big brother's waist and with a squeeze signaled he knew he would soon go.

Ashley smoothed his brother's hair, ran a thumb along his tear-streaked brow. And quickly, all too quickly, he felt the life of Willow Sutliff all at once remain and then, all forever recede.

Across the room, Ellery was groaning and trying to sit up. Julius went over to him, shooting a glance at Ashley. "We are compromised," he said, voice low, severe. "If the Brohms moved against us, that means the rest of the pack is moving against the McKennys."

"Carolina," moaned Hezekiah.

Ashley looked down into the long, seeing-nothing gaze of Willow. "They have to pay," he said. "We cannot let this stand."

Ellery shook his head, unable to comprehend where he was or how he had gotten there.

Julius put a hand on the young man's shoulder. "Can you stand?"

Ellery nodded, still trying to shake away the confusion. "I think so."

Julius stayed him. "Son, you are about to hear something terrible, but I need you to be strong now. I need you to hear and be strong."

His youngest brother turned, squinted at the body splayed across Ashley's lap, and his face paled, grew years older in an instant. "Will?"

"Your brother fought bravely, but he is gone," said Julius, squeezing Ellery's shoulder. "And if we do not run right now, the rest of us will die along with him. Do you understand?"

Ellery opened his mouth. He looked to Ashley. "Ashley?"

"Gone," said Ashley. And the hearts of the brothers Sutliff, now only two, collided. Across the world of that room, they broke together.

"On your feet, son," said Julius, helping Ellery to his feet. "Choke down your feelings. We have to run."

"Fuck running," said Ashley, carefully sliding his brother's broken body to the floor. "Fuck the Brohms and their people and their barony. I will make an end of them." The storm within him was swirling to tempest, hazarding all its rage-fueled strength in the hopes of becoming a hurricane.

"He is right," said Hezekiah. He stood near the bed, his clothes wet and red. "There is no victory to be found here. Only death. The Brohms have chosen war, and we are too little a company to throw any measure of strength against their power here."

Julius stepped toward Hezekiah, his pale skin like alabaster in the cold moonlight. "I will go to the pack leaders. Explain. Brohm will get his war."

"I will hide," said Ashley, slowly reloading

his pistol. "Wait for them to revert to their vulnerable form, kill them all where they stand."

"No," said Hezekiah. "They know your scent. There is nowhere to hide for you. The Brohms are about their business with the McKennys. Now is the only time to gather our horses, get away."

"So then, we won't hide," said Ellery, shakily stepping to the center of the room, closer to Willow.

It was the "we" that cast out all the fury from Ashley. He knew that for his sake and for that of revenge, Ellery would throw himself into the maelstrom that could claim them both. The fury of the storm subsided, dying away. "No," said Ashley, looking to his littlest brother. "We will get you and Willow to the stable. You must go back home. Mother needs you—more than ever. I will go with Julius. See our brother revenged."

Ellery balled his fists, grit his teeth and looked as imposing as any man Ashley had ever seen. "No," he said. "I will not leave. Let me come with you."

Ashley took a deep, sorrowful breath, remembering. He lifted his loaded revolver to aim it directly at Ellery. "Mother asked me to make sure you returned home. And so, little brother dearest, I will not ask at all."

Ellery Sutliff looked down the barrel of that pistol feeling never so betrayed, never loved more. Ashley wouldn't kill him, but he would shoot him, if he did not comply. Ashley had made a wager, pushed all-in to have his way, and Ellery had learned so long ago never to bet against his brother the gambler.

While Julius and Hezekiah went to the livery stable to fetch the horses, Ellery and Ashley wrapped the bodies of their beloved brother and Carolina in bedsheets. They worked quickly and carefully, staining the bedsheets with their tears. The night was quiet as they worked until, far off on the distant plains, came triumphant howls that so clearly resembled the Brohm howl they had heard.

They lifted the corpses onto their shoulders and carried them down the steps of the hotel, its little lobby empty of all life. Then, from the west came rushing hoofbeats. Julius was riding Carolina's Appaloosa with Martin and Ashley's gray tethered behind. Hezekiah had ditched the wagon and was riding his horse.

Ellery watched the horses come pounding up the otherwise empty thoroughfare.

"You tell mother I love her," said Ashley.

Ellery looked to Ashley. "You will tell her yourself."

"Hezekiah offered me a position with his company; I'm taking it. And until every single

Brohm is dead in the ground, I will not see home. So, you *will* tell mother I love her, Ellery. Take care of home and her, so that when my work is done, I can come back and tell her myself."

Julius, now dressed in a blood-soaked shirt and trousers taken from God knew where, pulled the horses to a stop. "If you're coming with me, now is the time to go," he said to Ashley.

They loaded Carolina's body onto the back of Hezekiah's horse and lashed it to the saddle.

"I failed you both," said Hezekiah. "I cannot ever make this loss up to you, but I swear to all that is, I will try." He turned to Ellery. "You're with me. Let's get you and Willow home."

Ashley and Julius lifted the bundle with Willow's body onto Martin's back.

"No," Ellery said. "You take Martin."

Ashley continued lashing the bundle onto the saddle. "You need all the speed you can get, little brother. And Martin belongs with his rider."

Ellery, having no arguments left within himself, merely said, "Yes, sir."

Ashley turned to face Ellery, and swallowed his brother in his arms. They embraced as though it would be the final time, neither of them knowing if that would be the truth of things.

"Please," said Ellery, the word failing to

convey the fullness of his wish. "Please come home."

Ashley squeezed him tight. "Take care of things while I'm gone."

"Only for a piece, brother." Ellery drew back to gaze once more upon his brother's face.

Ashley nodded, trying to hide all his fear and sadness and fury, though Ellery saw all its measure. "And only for a time."

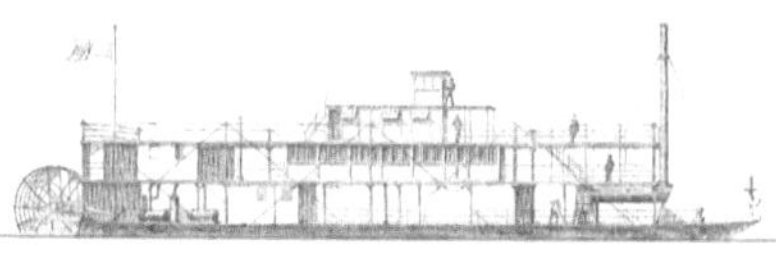

MARCH 15, 1845
CHICAGO, ILLINOIS

*D*ear Mother,

Hezekiah Ellison, or Judge Ellison as he insists we now call him, posted a letter from Les Pauvres l' atterrissage *to let me know that Ellery arrived home with Willow four days after the horror in the Little Kansas Barony. I have joined Judge Ellison's company alongside two others: an infamous knife fighter, Mary O'Shea, and a huckster who you would most certainly hate, Ollie Tapper. Julius Stephens is leading us until Judge Ellison finds his way here to Chicago. He sends his deepest regrets.*

I am sending my regrets, too.

But you already know that, Mother. It seems to me that now, living with my hard goodbye to Willow, that you might possibly know everything worth knowing. He saved my life. Died in my arms. My last words to him were an apology, and I will never get over it, because I should have apologized so much sooner for leaving as I did. That would have been best of me. That would have allowed my final words to my first little brother to be the 'I love you' he deserved.

I will never, ever get over it, Mother. Never.

He was so brave, and it was seeing his bravery that made me so sure we could conqueror the unconquerable. The look in his eyes. The determination writ across his face. His form robed in immense power. Carolina told us to run, but we failed to listen, and that cost Willow his life. Robbed you of your most dutiful son. And that is the true reason I waited to write.

I wanted to give you enough length of time to be disappointed with me, again. Give you the space of half-a-country and more than a whole month, so that your sadness for losing Daddy and your shock at losing your son could rise like a tide and, hopefully, ebb.

I told Stephens that very thing this morning over coffee. He said:

"You don't understand women at all."

I believe he is right. And in trying to understand, I began this letter to say just how sorry I am, at what an utter failure you worked so hard to raise up toward being a happy success. I am a failure, Mother. I failed as a son, a brother, a gambler, all.

Though I am a failure, I realize, because of you: That what I am now is not what I have to remain.

And so I have taken up with Judge Ellison and as his shootist, accompanying Julius Stephens, I will follow in the footsteps of my mother and her husband, my father, and I will seek out the Brohm brothers, all three. The lycanthropes have their ways, their customs, their laws. Their packs are split near down the middle when it comes to the destruction of the McKenny pack. And so, they will have their campaign, pack against pack, obeying the rules of conflict set by their den mothers and sire-line progenitors. That is how they will make war with each other. In their fashion.

I will make war with them in the human fashion.

This war will not be had in Missouri or the Little Kansas Barony or even the United States. The packs who supported the Brohms have gathered their wealth and kin and pushed westward to California, where already so much strife exists with tensions between Mexico and the Republic of Texas.

The Judge believes Texas will soon be annexed into the body of our country, and so he goes there for cheap land and a place to bury Carolina, so that she can forever be close by while he conducts his estate's mission.

I will go to California soon, Mother. Right now, in Chicago, my thoughts are wholly on you and Ellery, the home you are tending, and the loved ones buried on our acreage. But do not worry, for this letter is not a goodbye. I failed to write home while in St. Louis, and I will never fail you in that way again. I will post to you regularly as travel and circumstances allow. I will think of you every time I see the wild timberland, as I cross every hard-faced mountain, remembering how in so many ways I am just like you. And I will think of Daddy, too. I am trying to become the man he hoped I would grow into.

Give Ellery all my love, or at least as much of it as he is willing to accept. Insist that he not come join me, for I know he will try.

You were right, Momma. The goodbyes we say live with us forever. Change us. You were right about everything. I am certain you always will be. And I will be glad for your voice to fall upon my ear, telling me each and every way that while I was so wrong about so many things, I am right about this.

Tell Willow and Daddy that I love them each time you visit. Take care of our home, for I will see it again. You have my dying word as man and eternally as,

Your loving son,
Ashley Forrest Sutliff
Agent of the Peregrine Estate

About the Author

C.S. Humble is the award-winning American novelist of the Amid the Vastness of All Else Saga. He is also a screenplay and short story writer. He lives in East Texas.

A Note from Shortwave Publishing

Thank you for reading *To Carry a Body to Its Resting Place*! If you enjoyed this book, please consider writing a review. Reviews help readers find more titles they may enjoy, and that helps us continue to publish titles like this.

For more Shortwave titles, visit us online. . .

OUR WEBSITE
shortwavepublishing.com

SOCIAL MEDIA
@ShortwaveBooks

EMAIL US
contact@shortwavepublishing.com